Deron & Nariah

A Tarnished Tale Of Love

By: Shay Renee

It's easy to join our mailing list!

Just send your email address by text message:

Text

TMPBOOKS

to 22828 to get started.

Acknowledgments

I would like to express my appreciation to the many people who provided support, guidance, feedback, and assistance during the process of me writing this book. I have received so much love and encouragement throughout my journey, so it would only be right for me to return the favor and let you all know how much I truly value your honesty. With that being said, I would like to extend a special thank you to the following people....

I would like to thank my mother, Melissa St. Julien b.k.a. Authoress Lady Lissa, for pushing me and keeping me focused at all times. She always saw the best in me, looked for ways to increase my potential, and inspired me in more ways than I can count. I love her with everything in me, and I am extremely thankful to have such an amazing author as a mother.

I would like to thank my daughter Aubree Alexander, my sister Trinity St. Julien, and my fiancé Jarred Alexander, for being my motivation and encouraging me to become the author I never thought I could be.

I would like to give a special thank you to Maria Harrison and Tiece Mickens for always being there for me. They made themselves available to me whenever I needed them and I truly appreciate that.

I would also like to give a special thank you to Bryant Sparks for going above and beyond my expectations and designing the perfect cover for my story.

I would like to give a shout out to the many authors who have encouraged and supported me: Alexus Dominique, Christine Chrissy J. Joyner, Dabinique

Magwood, Falana Betts, Andre James Carter, Authoress Destiny, Author Renee Hill, Tisha Andrews, Annika Grace, Quardeay Julien, Lola Bandz, Author Nicole Shephard, Mesha Turner, Solisa Marie, Tiffany McGee, Author Bernadette Whatley, Kimberlaine Johnson, Marquita-Rogers Cross, Kandy Kaine, Tanaijsa Brutus, T'Ann Marie, Tranay Adams, Sa'id Salaam, Sabrina Weaver, Xachari A. Morgan, Shatika Turner, Jasmine Devonish, Tracy Williams, Teruka B. Carey, Author Valarie DeShazier, Yatta Rose, Rae Bae, Author Asar, Diamond Stanford, Tia Barnes, Tselyn Hinton Vs Turner, Lucy Dee, Nileyah Rose, LaRissa Robinson, Shelli Marie, Briana Mills, Tela Allen, Christine Chrissy Love, Kisha K'Vonne Reinhardt, Rere Mebby, Kashley Brown, Wayne Moore, Leondra LeRae, Shaunda Renee, Willie Leblanc, Drea Delgado, Myia White, Latitta Waggoner, Tracey Knight, Kia Meche, Authoress Caramel Cocayne, Trinity DeKane, Bryan Ambitious, Author Christaviyahs, Authoress Shante, Jennifer Holliman, Shanicia Jackson, Carde'l Edens, Tra'von Williams, Belinda Harvey, Naporcha Dion, Author Jason Beckett, Brittany Alexander, Angela Miller, Malika Dews, Jennel Krystal Armstead, Author Shaniya Dennis, Qiana L. Dior, Monique Hill, Vivian Blue, Authoress K. Marquelle, Author KF Johnson, Denetria Gibson, Charles Burgess, Candies Williams, and last but not least Neka Franklin.

I would also like to give a shout out to the many readers who has been rocking with me since day one: Shonnikkia Francois, Tanya Hypolite, Christine Williams, Lisa Barney, Pat Pillette, Brandy Landrio, Kenry Green, Shae Cunningham, Tim Etienne, Luci Tucci, Angel Denise, Shirra Mines, Renee Watson, Reginald Ross, Teri Blakely, Tanya Wiles, Shekie Johnson, Chele Council, Shaquana

Alfred, Ray Junior, Daphine Marcus, Helen Richard,
Daisha Hall, Danielle Thompson, Angela Smith, Shalana
Chargois Francis, Elizabeth Schult, Eulana Breaux,
Taniesha Lacy, Cheyenne Rivera, Tywanna Cummings,
Tonya Mouton, Lakisha Rankin, Tiara Sullins, Kimberly
Davis, Latoya Samuel, Diana Waldo, Cassandra Williams,
Teneisha Huff, Kodi Tauzin, Bryanna Smith, CandyAnn
Ferris, Taleighta Carter, Jiaymeta Moore, Lakivya Henson,
Tiffany Strickland Stelly, Melissa Gabriel, Tae'Cheka
Sabille, Tawana William's, Tara Wells, Shawanda Woods,
Alexandria Ponce, Asia Shanae', Asmahah Edwards,
Regina Boutte, Yolanda Williams, Asia Phillip, Jeannette
Ransom-Frazier, Latanya Burress, Alania Henson-
Rossyion, Brandie Shields, Patricia Reid, Dorothea
Creamer, Jeanea Cooper, Shawda Love, Tammy Jones,
Keyette Joiner, Artesure Johnson, Martia Clark, Rochelle
Denise, Carol Mustipher, Tria Burnett, Dee Williams, Kim
Chatman, Kipper Blue, Yajiida Jackson, Rochelle Pettrie,
Nicole Alford-Pollard, Tiffany Monique, Anita Wade, Joan
Brooks, A.J. Jeanine, Camry Hunter, Luciana Royster,
Seneca Steven, Demetrius Marsalis, Tameshia Noel,
Tamicka Strickland Roberts, Charolette Thomas-Gurley,
Tanessia Ford, Quaran Owens, Deilra Smith-Collard,
Nicole Mckinley, Candy Roy, Jessica Pitts, Kitani
Quoweya Jedae Martin, Jacqueline D. Thomas, Angela
Hayes Taylor, Tonja Williamson, Nicole Davis, Linda Hall,
Pamela Johnston Ward, Rodnesha Jones, Theresa Joseph,
Wee Williams, Iesha Barnes, Sweets Gray, Jennifer Jones,
Christina Hull, Sheila Sales Brown, Ella Warren, Cleo D.
Paris, Jessie Joseph, Glenda Coats, Goldie Love, Jacole
Laryea, Jalisa Dear, Geraldine Etienne, Eric Robert,
Shaneka Johnson, Shanice Horton, Bianca Edmond, Shelly
Glaude, Anna Walker, Karen Touchet, Angie Love, Letisha

Williams, Christy Hypolite, Spring Skyy, Brian Dural, Amanda Linton, Natalie Ann Adams, Jojuana Wilkins, Linda Ellis, Natasscia Shelvin, Tymeisha Wright-Russ, Joshua Sean Johnson, Christina Reyna, Christian Joseph, Sandra Boykin, Jess Hubbard, S.T. Sneed, Brandy Bowden, Randell Scott, Juju Brown, Lisa Amos Landry, Andrew Fennell, Mark Deas, John Pena, Jae Bee, Kendra Stearns, Teidra Banks-Fontenette, Rebecca Alexander, LaTonza Jamison-Herring, Jasmine Joseph, Stacy Noel Calais, Delayna Jackson, Chrissie Tatman-Dotson, JoAnn Hunter-Scott, Brittany Kilcrease, Paula Milan, Ro Shaw, Kaiata Moore, Nanita Barrett, Dorian Walker, Maya Bell, Mya Robinson, A'Marie Walls, Amerie Perez, An-Janette Albert, Jasmine Ealey, Crystal Samuel, Tanya Gary, Sympa Ladii, Shar S. Mobley, Denise Roy, Nicole Prejean, Roxanne Arceneaux-Alexander, Darren Coleman, Shamiya Falke-Barnett, Ray Junior, Chas Grier, Paula Murphy, JeaNida Weatherall, Avante Gabriel, Abreanna Alexander, Rochelle Andrews, Saderia Green, Tootie Williams, and last but not least Kendra Reeves.

If I have failed to mention someone, I am truly sorry and I hope you can forgive me. This journey has been long, and I am forever grateful for having each and every one of you by my side through it all. Thank you again.

Prologue - Deron

Watching Nariah walk away was one of the worst feelings I have ever experienced. Now I ain't gon' sit here and act like I didn't know what I was doing, cuz I did. And I won't even try to play the victim like I'm not wrong, cuz I am. But I didn't think she'd go out and retaliate.

Honestly, if I knew that me cheating would have eventually led to this, I would've quit a long time ago. Yea, I know that you're probably saying I deserve it, and I do. But that doesn't make me hurt any less. I've felt pain before, but this type of pain is one I'm not used to. I guess us niggas really can't take what we dish out. Cuz right now, I don't have the mentality or the strength to just accept the fact that my woman opened her legs to another nigga. Then to hear that she's pregnant for him. Man, that shit is hard to stomach. What makes it worse, is knowing that my actions caused this. I really don't know what to do at this point, but what I do know is that I have to find a way to get my better half back.

About an hour after Nariah drove off, I pulled out my phone to hit up my bro Nick. At a time like this, he was the only person I knew that I could vent to. He knew a lot about this relationship shit, so maybe he could help me figure out what to do.

I searched for his number in my contacts and hit call. To my surprise, he answered on the fourth ring. Usually he'd pick up as soon as the phone started ringing, so that kinda had me worried.

"What up baby brother?" he answered.

"Coolin bro. What took you so long to pick up? A nigga could've been dying or trapped behind a squad car."

Nick let out a slight chuckle. "Quit buggin bro. I was in here handling some business before I head to the city. You know how I do. What's up with you though? What you got going on?"

"Mannnn, it's all bad son. Me and shawty just got into it and she bounced. She found out about the baby, and shit just exploded after that. She had DNA results and everything, so my back was against the wall."

"Yo word? How she get the test results bro? Don't you gotta go through all kinda legal shit to get that info?"

"Yea, but Allyson dumb ass had them mailed to the crib. She got to the mailbox before I did and was reading them bitches when I pulled up."

Before I could say anything else, there was a moment of silence. A few seconds later, I began to hear a familiar voice in the background. It kinda sounded like my girl, but I wasn't sure. I probably was just trippin, but something was telling me I wasn't.

"Say bro, you got company?" I asked in a serious tone.

"Oh, yea bro. Uh, one of my lil issues popped up on me a minute ago. Matter of fact, let me hit you back in about 2 hours," he said while rushing off the phone.

Chapter One - Nariah

Growing up in Houston, there's nothing I hadn't seen. Murders, drug deals, escorting, I had been around it all. At the tender age of 14, my mother became a drug addict after my father passed away. To add insult to injury, she kicked my older sister Laya out a week later for refusing to give her money so that she could get high. She wouldn't let me leave with her, so after that I was pretty much on my own. With Laya out of the house and my mother being high all of the time, I had to step up and learn how to care for myself.

I had to wash my own clothes, clean the house, cook when we had food, take care of my mother when she got sick, and keep up with the bills all while going to school. There were plenty of times where I went to bed hungry and had to bathe in cold water due to the electricity being turned off. We also ended up homeless for a couple of months, and had to sleep in shelters and even under overpasses when the shelters were full. When the school found out what was going on, child services were called and I was removed out of my mother's care. The state placed me in a group home until my aunt was granted custody of me, but living with her was like living inside of a horror movie.

My aunt only took me in for the check, so she wasn't really a motherly figure. She made me do everything that she didn't want to do, which at times included sleeping with her husband against my will. Every time he got paid, she sent me upstairs to her bedroom. I couldn't put up a fight or tell anyone, because she would always threaten to send me back to the group home. One day after school, I got ahold of her cell phone and called my mother to let her know what had been going on. My mother ended up coming over that night to confront my aunt and take me back home with her, but things didn't go as planned.

Instead of inviting her in, they spoke to her through the door and offered her money and drugs to leave. However, as tempting as it was, my mother refused to take anything from them and continued to beg for me. When they saw that she wasn't going to give up, they both went outside to try to scare her away. A couple of minutes later, there was a lot of screaming, followed by gun shots. I ran from my room to see what was happening, but neither my aunt nor her husband would allow me to step outside of the house.

I ran to the sofa and opened the curtains in the living room, only to see my mother laid out on the sidewalk bleeding from her chest. I think I may have passed out at the sight of her lifeless body, because the only thing I remembered after that is waking up in a hospital bed surrounded by police. Long story short, my aunt and her husband ended up going to jail and I ended up going back to the group home where I was forced to stay until I turned twenty-one.

*****

Three years later, I graduated from the Art Institute of Houston with a Bachelor's degree of Fine Arts in Fashion Design and working for one of the top designers in the city, STYLECIRCLE. I was also living in my own luxury apartment, and pushing a 2016 Honda Accord EX. I was doing really well for myself compared to where I had come from, but all of that changed when I met Deron.

"Yo ma," I heard someone yell as I walked to my car.

I had just finished dropping off a set of classic pinstripe prints to my job. I was up all night making sure that everything was perfect and in order, so I really wasn't in the mood to socialize. I kept walking, but was suddenly stopped in my tracks. The guy who was yelling was now parked right next to me. He opened the door and stepped out of the car.

"You can't speak?"

I scanned him up and down with a disinterested look on my face. He was cute as hell and looked very familiar, but I didn't recall ever seeing him here before. He stood about 6'1, 180 pounds with a taper fade cut, a neatly shaved goatee, and a smooth ass skin complexion with just a tad bit of acne. He was basically a life size Ken doll, but with a hood boy swag. The only thing that turned me off about him was the way he approached me. I unlocked my doors and looked over my shoulder.

"I was taught not to speak to strangers."

He smiled and rubbed his hands together. "I don't have to be a stranger, ma. I'm actually trying to change that if it's cool with you."

I flipped my hair and rolled my eyes. "Yelling at me from across the parking lot isn't a way to get a lady's attention."

He gawked and put his hand on his chin. His shocked expression almost made me laugh. I could tell that he wasn't used to getting rejected, but he still didn't give up.

"Damn. You're right though love and I apologize. How about we start over? I'm Deron, and I'm interested in getting to know you, if that's cool with you beautiful."

I bowed my head, letting my hair hit my face. Something told me to just listen to my gut and get in my car, but another part of me wanted to know more about him. I extended my arm out to shake his hand.

"Nice to meet you, Deron. I'm Nariah."

He gently grasped my hand. "I'm sorry ma. Your name is Na what?"

"It's Nariah, like Mariah."

"I heard you the first time love, but you said it so sexy I just had to hear you say it again. That's a beautiful name, Nariah."

I blushed and pulled my hand back. "Thank you."

"So Nariah, do you mind if we exchange numbers and talk sometime? I'm kind of in a rush right now. I usually don't do this, but that pretty face of yours caught my attention so I just had to speak."

Looking at the kind of car he was driving and how he was dressed, I knew exactly what he meant by being in a rush. He was in a fully loaded, 2016 white Dodge Challenger with 22" white and black spoke rims, and tinted windows, wearing basketball shorts and a wife beater. Everything about him screamed drug dealer, but at the same time, the only kind of men who came through here were high profile business men, so maybe he was legit. I guess it wouldn't hurt to give him a chance. After all, my nights were starting to get pretty lonely.

"I guess we could do that."

He pulled out his phone and handed it to me. I keyed in my number, then gave it back to him. "Next time, don't be so arrogant."

I got in my car and drove off. I wasn't trying to come off as a snobby bitch, but I had to let him know what type of woman he was dealing with. I wasn't like the around the way thots he was probably used to. I was far from your average female, so if a nigga wanted to step to me he had to know how to address me and "yo ma" just didn't cut it.

When I finally got home, it was 7:23 pm. I had literally been on the road all day running errands and securing my bag. I was beyond exhausted and ready to call it a night, but I still had one last thing to do. I reached inside of my purse and pulled out my mail. I had been waiting for a copy of my transcripts from the Art Institute of Houston for weeks now, but just as I expected it still hadn't come in.

I threw the mail down on the bar, picked up my purse, and headed upstairs to hop in the shower. Usually, I'd pour myself a glass of wine and relax with a book from one of my favorite authors, but I was too tired to drink or read tonight. Before I could gather my robe and head to the bathroom, I heard the familiar sound of Wiz Khalifa's latest release, Something New, coming from my phone. This was odd, because no one ever called me after 5 pm. I picked up my phone off of the bed to see who it was, but I didn't recognize the number.

"Hello."

"What's up beautiful? I hope I ain't catch you at a bad time," the unfamiliar voice said.

I looked at my phone and smiled. I knew exactly who it was, but I couldn't let him know that. You're never supposed to let a nigga know that you're waiting for his call, his time, or anything else that he has to offer. If you do, you'll always be treated like an option. You must always make them make you a priority.

I sat on the bed and crossed my legs.

"No, you didn't catch me at a bad time. But may I ask who this is?"

"My bad boo, this Deron. May I please speak to Nariah?"

Now that was more like it.

"Oh, hey. I wasn't expecting you to call this late." I responded. "I was actually about to hop in the shower and get ready for bed. What's going on with you? Sounds like you're having a party."

"Nah love. Ain't no party going on here yet. I'm just chillin at my potna's club right now. I got some shit to handle in the morning, so I ain't really trying to do too much. It would be nice if I could see you though."

"You wanna see me?" I asked surprisingly.

"Yea, I wanna see you. What's wrong with that? You don't want me to see you? I know you're probably looking all good and shit like you was earlier."

"Actually, I look the exact same way I did earlier. I not too long ago got home. I just told you I was about to get in the shower," I laughed.

"Shiddd, earlier you looked like a snack. Had a nigga mouth all watery and shit."

Deron really had me sitting there with butterflies in my stomach, which was extremely rare. Normally, I was cold with these niggas, but for some strange reason with him it was different. It was almost as if we'd known each other for years, and we hadn't even known each other for a full 24-hours. I held the phone closer to my ear.

"Just imagine how I look on my best days," I flirtatiously responded.

"Well look, how about you hop in the shower, get your Beyoncé on, and meet up with me at the club? I'll shoot you the address and you can pull up. We can talk over a few drinks and get to know one another a little better. How does that sound?"

I really wanted to say yes, but I knew I had to work in the morning. We were preparing for a huge fashion presentation and I had to be there early to deliver another set of prints. My boss had already been riding my back after another designer got a hold of one of our portfolios last month, so I had to show up and show out.

"As much as I would love too, I'll have to decline. I have to work in the morning, but maybe we can hook up another time," I responded.

"I feel that, but listen love, I would never put you in a position where you could possibly lose your job. I promise if you come, you'll be back home before Cinderella loses her glass slipper," he laughed.

This man truly had a way with words, which made it hard for me to stick to my first mind. I didn't want to risk losing my job, but all I ever did was work and come home. I didn't really have any friends, except for the few co-workers I occasionally hooked up with, so my life was rather boring. Going out to mingle a bit didn't sound too bad, and was something that was long overdue. As long as I got at least five hours of sleep, I'd be fine.

I uncrossed my legs and lied back on the bed. "Okay. I guess I can slide through for a couple of minutes, but I can't stay for longer than an hour."

"Square bidness. I'm 'bout to shoot you the address now, and you can just hit my line when you're on your way. And aye, wear something sexy for me."

I laughed and ran my fingers through my hair. "I'll see what I can put together."

We spoke for a few more minutes, then said our goodbyes and ended the call. A minute later, I received a text from him with the address to the club. When I pulled up the location on Google, I noticed that it was actually a popular strip club named ONYX. I guess that explained where all the noise was coming from. I put my phone on the charger, picked up my things, and headed to the bathroom. I didn't know what tonight had in store, but I was curious to find out.

*****

When I was done taking my shower, I went to my closet and picked out a nice Bodycon dress that would show off my curves. I wasn't the smallest female in the world, so when it came down to stepping out, I had to make sure that I killed shit every time. Don't get me wrong, I was blessed in all the right places. I stood at 5'5, 162 pounds, size C-cup breasts, had a semi flat stomach, a nice set of hips, and a round plump ass to match. I also had a beautiful milk chocolate complexion, defined cheekbones, and straight pearly white teeth.

My body was banging, but to the people who didn't appreciate thickness I was considered to be on the fat side. Hell, I didn't care. As long as my pockets stayed as fat as my ass, what they thought would always mean nothing.

After I got dressed, I went back into the bathroom to do my hair and makeup. I didn't really care for foundation, but NARS Matte lipstick, Kholiner, and Audacious mascara were my go to beauty tools.

I was a sucker for smoky eyes and bold lips, and I wasn't ashamed to admit it. When I was done doing my face, I grabbed a few bobby pins and pinned my hair up in a messy bun. It didn't make sense for me to straighten it when I didn't plan on being out for longer than an hour. I preferred the natural look anyway; my curls never failed me. Once I was done beating my face and slaying my hair, I sprayed a little of my Bath & Body Works Pretty as a Peach body spray on my wrists and neck, then headed out.

I shot Deron a text to let him know that I was on my way, then put on my GPS. I was really looking forward to seeing him but at the same time, I was nervous as hell. I hadn't been on a date in years. Not because I wasn't getting any play, but because I was focused on getting and keeping my shit together. I sacrificed a lot to get to where I am now, and I refused to allow myself to fall on my ass and end up back in the hood.

Those days of living like an inmate were over. Besides, once my mom died, I promised to never go back there again. I plugged my phone up to the USB and turned on my Bluetooth. I scrolled through my playlist and stopped on 21 Savage's new song Bank Account. I know you're probably wondering what do I know about that, but 2 Chainz said it best, pretty girls like trap music. I turned the volume up as loud as it could go and took off.

I made it to the club a little after 9:00 pm. When I finally found somewhere to park, I sent Deron another text to let him know that I was outside. I waited a few minutes to see if he'd reply back before I attempted to go inside, but he didn't.

"I hope this nigga didn't stand me up," I said to myself while looking around the parking lot. For a Thursday night, this bitch was packed. I mean, cars lined up on side of the street packed. Even the handicapped spaces were full. It really looked like Popeye's on a Tuesday, to be honest. I don't know what the special occasion was, but if Deron didn't hit me up soon I was leaving. I made it clear before I left that I didn't have time to waste.

A few more minutes passed, and this nigga still hadn't replied. I put my car in reverse, and was about to leave until I saw my phone begin to light up. Before I could answer, there was a knock on my window. I grabbed my taser out of the glove box before I rolled down the window. I wasn't familiar with this side of town, and if I had to fry a motherfucker I would. When I rolled down the window, Deron was standing there smiling, but when he saw the taser his eyes lit up.

"You was tryna leave me ma, and what the hell you doing with that?" He asked looking confused.

"I've been sitting out here alone for over ten minute's texting you. You wasn't replying, so yes I was about to leave. You told me to text you before I left and I did, so you should've been waiting for my message or at least waiting outside," I replied.

"My bad. I ain't hear my phone go off cuz it's noisy as fuck in the building. I should've been looking out for you, but in my defense though, I can't just let nobody catch me wandering around outside no strip club. Plus a fight broke out, so I couldn't really move around how I wanted to," he explained. "But what the hell are you doing with a taser?"

"I didn't know who was knocking on my window, so I wanted to make sure I could defend myself if something popped off. And how are we gonna talk inside of a noisy ass strip club anyway? And if you're so worried about someone catching you outside, why did you invite me here in the first place?"

"These hoes ain't gon' touch you shawty, believe that. And I got a spot sectioned off especially for us, so you ain't even gotta worry about all the noise. I'm sorry if I let you down love. At least give me a chance to show you better than I can tell you," he replied with a smile.

I put my car back in park, rolled up my window, and turned the car off. In a way, I guess I was kind of overreacting. Maybe it was because I wasn't used to this type of date. I rarely went out, and I for damn sure didn't do strip clubs. I took off my seat belt and opened the door. When I stepped out, he backed up and leaned against the car.

"Damn ma," Deron said as he bit his bottom lip.

I gave him a puzzled look before checking out my reflection in the window.

"Is something wrong?"

I knew that nothing was wrong, but I just wanted to make sure I was legit before stepping foot inside of the club. This was one of the many places you couldn't get caught looking a mess in. Rappers, athletes, and other A-list celebrities were always in Houston, and they were always getting spotted at a strip club. Being that I worked in the fashion industry, I couldn't afford to get caught slipping and end up on the Z-list. After what happened with Florence earlier, I needed to protect the few pieces of my career that I still had left.

Deron stood there staring at me like I was a scoop of his favorite ice cream.

"Ain't shit wrong girl, you look amazing. But you'd look even better on my arm."

I looked up at him to see that his eyes were now glued to my ass. He took my hand and pulled me closer to him. When he wrapped his arm around my waist, I instantly felt my body melt. This nigga looked and smelled good as hell. He had on a black pair of Levi jeans, a cream colored Polo Ralph Lauren collar shirt, with the matching Polo Ralph Lauren Vaughn casual sneakers, and a gold Cuban link chain to compliment his look. Just looking at him made me want to say fuck the club. I didn't want to come off as easy though, so I just smiled and played it cool.

Deron then leaned over my shoulder and whispered in my ear. "You ready to go in?"

If we weren't outside, I honestly believe I would've came out of my dress and got to twerking. This nigga had my legs feeling like Mama Noodles and my pussy on Dasani. I had to find a way to contain the freak in me, and I needed to do it fast. I didn't even know his full name yet. Hell, I didn't even know if Deron was even his real name. I pulled away from him and pretended to check my hair again. Once my fire was out, I reached for his hand.

"Now we can go in now. Do they accept credit cards? Cuz I don't have any more cash and I forgot to stop to the ATM on the way here."

He looked at me and laughed.

"What's funny? I'm serious."

"Nothing love. You're good. Everything for you is covered. I even have a couple bands for you to throw if you're into that kind of stuff," he replied.

"Thanks, but I'll leave all the throwing up to you."

I honestly didn't give a damn about throwing money at no stripper bitches. The only thing that was on my mind was throwing this ass back at him. We walked across the parking lot, skipped the line, and entered the club. As we walked through the club, I was speechless. It was my first time being in this type of environment, so all I could do was stare.

ONYX was nothing like the clubs they showed on t.v. There was pussy and ass everywhere I turned. Deron was bobbing his head and glowing like a kid in a candy store, but I on the other hand was a little uncomfortable. The only naked ass I liked looking at was my own, but I couldn't let him see that I wasn't feeling the scenery. I didn't want to kill the vibe.

Once we got through the crowd, Deron led me to our section and made sure to keep a tight grip on my hand. I had eyes on me from every angle of the building, so that was his way of letting these other niggas know that I was off limits. When we made it to our section, I let out a huge sigh of relief.

"Nariah, you good boo?" Deron asked while opening up a bottle of Moet champagne.

"I'm fine," I lied. "I'm just trying to take all of this in. I've never been to a strip club before, so it's just like wow. I see why marriages don't last these days."

He smiled as he poured up a drink.

"Yea, shit can get kind of wild in here at times. But it's chill right now. The fun starts after midnight."

He handed me the glass, and I kindly declined. I know I agreed to talk over drinks, but after looking around I realized that I needed to do my best to stay alert. I didn't want to get fucked up and put myself in a vulnerable position.

"You don't drink champagne?" he asked while setting the drink down.

"Yea, but I have to work in the morning remember? Plus, I have to drive back home."

"One drink won't hurt love. You gon' be straight by the time you get ready to leave. Being that we only got an hour together, I want to make sure you enjoy yourself while you're here. Loosen up a bit and just unwind for a minute. I know you're a hard working woman, and I respect that. But every woman needs a break at some point to just be themselves, and live a little."

He was right. I was a very hard working woman, which is why I didn't want to drink. I worked damn near six days a week, and clocked in 16 to 18 hours a day in the studio working on the next hot piece. Lord knows I was beyond tired of seeing designs, but that's how I ate and survived. I couldn't mess that up.

I looked over and noticed that Deron was sitting there with a blank expression on his face. I was terrible at this dating thing and I more than sure it showed. I picked up the glass off of the table and held it up in the air.

"One drink. That's it."

Chapter Two – Deron

Nariah was looking good as hell in that lil short ass dress she had on. I could tell she was trying to play the holy moly shy girl role, but I could see right pass that shit. She wasn't like the rest of these hoes, but she wasn't a saint either.

"One drink it is then, baby." I replied as I poured me up a glass of Henny.

I wasn't trying to get too fucked up tonight either, but I had a lot on my mind. Niggas was starting to run their mouths about what I had going on, and it was starting to fuck with my career. One thing I hated was a snake as nigga, especially one that interfered with my money. I looked over at Nariah, who was sitting there looking out at one of the dancers on stage. The look on her face told me that she liked that kind of shit. It just took the right nigga to bring it out of her. And that nigga was me.

"So what's up love?" I asked while looking into her eyes.

"Nothing. I'm trying to learn a few of these moves, and see what's up with you," she playfully replied.

"Oh yea? Shit, it ain't hard to learn. Whenever you wanna practice just say the word and let me know. When I'm not busy getting to the money, I got you."

She sat her drink down and turned to me.

"What exactly do you mean by getting to the money? What is your profession?"

I knew that this question was coming. I hated telling females what I did cuz once they found out shit always went left. I took my drink to the head and faced her. "I'm a basketball player baby. I'm the starting point guard for the Houston Rockets, and your favorite player's biggest competition."

I didn't go into detail about what I did on the side, cuz I ain't wanna scare shawty away. This was our first lil date, if that's what you wanna call it, so some shit just didn't need to be discussed right away. In time, she would find out exactly how I moved on and off of the court. Maybe she could even become the partner that I needed. I lived a very public life, so I needed a woman that would be open to doing the same or at least be understanding of what I did in private. I wasn't tryna give up what I built outside of basketball just yet.

"Wow, I knew you looked familiar. I was trying to remember where I had seen your face, but I just couldn't figure it out. But that's nice. Maybe I can come to one of your games one day."

I looked at Nariah with a grin from ear to ear. She was the first female who didn't go insane when I told her that I played ball. Usually, these other hoes would get all excited and start asking me a million questions, but she didn't and I loved that about her.

"Sounds good, but enough about me, I'm trying to see what's good with you. I like what I'm seeing, and I'm truly digging the vibe between us right now. I hope we can get closer and work on getting to know each other without the bullshit and the games," I responded while gazing into her eyes.

She picked up her drink and finished it.

"That would be cool. I don't mind getting to know you, as long as you don't have any baggage or crazy people behind you. I know the groupies be falling all over you, and I'm not trying to be no team player."

"You would be the only one Nariah. I'm not with all that fucking around and sneaky shit. They got too much shit being passed around for all that, plus I'm a very private person when I'm not in the limelight. I can't get caught up in no type of scandal. Any and everything I do affects the whole team, so I'm always on my best behavior baby."

Nariah laughed and shook her head. The champagne must've been getting to her, cuz her eyes were starting to look a lil low and she was starting to rock back and forth. I could already see how this night was about to play out. She was enjoying herself, but I knew that if I didn't refill her glass she would eventually get to guilt trippin and whining about work. I wasn't trying to hear that shit all night.

I picked up the bottle of champagne out of the bucket and poured her another drink.

Nariah pushed her finger into my chest. "We agreed on one glass."

"Relax baby. You'll be aight. It's only 10:07 pm."

She leaned over and put her head on my chest. "But I have to work tomorrow, and I can't be late."

Nariah was starting to slur. If this is what a glass of champagne did to her, I'd hate to see what would happen if she drank something harder. I put my arm around her back and rubbed her side.

"Baby girl, you gon be aight. I promise. Just trust me. My word is bond."

As Nariah picked up the drink and slowly began to sip again, my phone vibrated in my pocket and made her jump. I slid my arm from behind her to see who was texting me. It was my bro Nick. I had to meet him in the back of the club to handle some shit. I stood up and looked at Nariah.

"Love, I gotta excuse myself for a few minutes. I won't be long though. I just need to holla at my bro real fast."

She stood up and placed her hand on her hip.

"So you're just gonna leave me here by myself?"

"Nah, I ain't leaving the club. I'll just be in the back for a second handling something. But as soon as I'm done, I'll come right back to you," I replied. "I promise I won't be long."

She downed her glass, then sat back down and poured her up another drink. I knew she wasn't going nowhere, cuz her ass was almost to the point to where she wouldn't be able to drive. I kissed her on her forehead and made my way around to the back of the club. When I got there, Nick was already standing by the dressing room waiting for me.

"What up blood?" he asked.

"Nothing fam. What's good? You got the shipment right?" I responded while dapping him up.

"Hell yea I got the shipment. But look bro, shit starting to get rocky at the pickup site. When I pulled up, there was a black Charger just sitting off in the cut. I had to get my man to follow me around to another spot just to be on the safe side. I think somebody talking bro, and we don't need that. YOU definitely don't need that."

I stood against the wall and shook my head. I already knew what he was talking about. One of my homies had already laced me up about the mysterious Charger. Shit was getting crazy, and that's why I needed Nariah by my side. I couldn't risk getting caught up, especially with the reporters always on my ass.

I needed something to do or somebody to flaunt to always have an alibi. I pulled out a ring box from my back pocket and opened it, exposing a gold key.

"Yea bro, I heard about that shit. Yo, I don't know what the fuck going on but we can't be having all that. But look, I got a shawty that I met earlier waiting for me in V.I.P. I'm tryna see what's up with her and shit, so we gotta do this as fast as possible."

I handed the key to Nick.

"Just put everything where it goes, and grab your package from the spot I showed you last time. Allyson should be in the dressing room waiting, so you shouldn't have no problems doing what you gotta do. Once everything is everything, just shoot me a text so I can get shit moving. I'll hit your line in the morning when I get back from practice, so we can finish handling business. Be safe out there bro," I stated while walking away.

Nick nodded his head and took off to the dressing room. Something was up with the way he mentioned the car at the pickup. I wasn't really too concerned about them being there, cuz everybody knew what came with fucking over me. But his demeanor was most certainly questionable. It's like he knew more than what was being said, but my brother had never crossed me before, so I really ain't had shit to worry about. If anything, the one I'd need to watch was Allyson.

Allyson was the first stripper that I met when I started playing ball. When I got drafted almost a year ago, Nick decided to throw a yacht party in Galveston and invite a few dancers; she was one of them. We kicked it at the party, had a nightcap, and exchanged numbers. A couple of weeks after that we hooked back up and kicked it for a few months.

We even tried to date each other, but she started trippin and getting too comfortable. This chick started popping up at practice, causing scenes at my games, and she even started letting herself into my crib when I wasn't home. We ended up falling out a few months later, which was also around the same time she called me and said she was leaving her parents' house behind some crazy shit with her stepdad. At first I didn't care, but when she showed up at my door crying with all her shit I felt bad for her and allowed her to stay with me until she got on her feet. When

I started doing my shit on the side, I needed somewhere to conduct my business and someone to help with the drop-offs.

Since I was giving her somewhere to lay her head, Allyson agreed to help me out and do it at the club under the condition that we continued to fuck. At first I wasn't with it, cuz her shit wasn't all that. But once I saw the money that was coming in, I guess you could say I had a change of heart. I made it back to the V.I.P. section just in time to stop Nariah from falling to the floor. She was fucked up and leaning all over the place. Seeing her like that kinda fucked my head up. I should've listened when she said one drink.

"Nariah, you straight?" I asked while pushing her up.

She opened her eyes a little and looked at me with a slight smirk.

"I ok. I just, I just…"

Nariah suddenly leaned forward and threw up directly on my Jordans. Shawty was officially out of there.

"Damn, yo. Get up baby girl. I need to get you out of here and take you home."

"I can driveeeee," she replied.

"Nah, you can't drive shit, ma." I stated while scooping her up. She had me fucked up if she thought I was about to let her get behind the wheel. The last thing I needed is a death on my hands. I spotted one of my teammates sitting across from us in a nearby section and gave him a signal to let him know that I was bouncing. On my way out of the door, I bumped into one of the dancers that Allyson be running with it. I knew that she was gonna run back and let Allyson know that I was leaving with a female, so I decided to send her ass back with a message.

"Yo Lexi, let your girl know that I'm out. Tell her to get Kayla to drive her car home, so she can drive mine. I gotta get this girl home," I stated while handing her my car keys.

Lexi sighed and shook her head. "You're still at it huh? I guess you really can't keep your dick in your pants. But whatever, I'll let her know."

I nodded my head and kept walking. I hated talking to that lil' sexy bitch. She had a smart ass mouth, but knew exactly what she was doing with it. I remember having to take her ass home quite a few times behind Allyson's back, and if I wasn't there with Nariah I probably would've stuck around to see if she needed a ride. It's been a minute since I got some sloppy top from her, and no lie, I kinda missed it.

Out of nowhere, Nariah picked her head up and started looking around.

"Who'sssss Allysonnn?" she asked still slurring.

"She ain't nobody important. She's one of the bitches that work here who handles business for me when shit comes up. I need her to drive my car, so I can take you home. I can't let you get on the road by yourself like this." I replied. "Give me your keys, so I can unlock the doors."

She reached into her bra and handed me her keys and her phone. I placed her phone in my pocket, then unlocked the doors and slid her in the passenger seat. I went around and got in the driver's seat, and shot Allyson a text before pulling off. I had to make sure that Lexi delivered my message before I left. She wasn't really the type of stripper that could be trusted. Her ass operated like Ronnie from The Player's Club.

When Allyson texted me back and said that shit was cool, I started Nariah's car and drove off. I tried to wake her up to get her address, but she wouldn't budge. I didn't wanna take this girl to my crib, but I couldn't just go drop her off at a room either. The end result would be bad publicity.

"Fuck it," I said to myself while getting on the highway.

I was just gonna have to bite the bullet, and take her home with me. Hopefully, she wouldn't wake up spazzing out and shit thinking a nigga was trying to do something to her. I got on the tollway and sped all the way to my crib. I didn't wanna be seen driving this girl's car, especially with her on the passenger side all fucked up. If that happened, I wouldn't be able to explain shit to coach. My ass would automatically be benched for the next five games.

I made it to my crib in less than twenty minutes. I was pushing the fuck out of her Honda. I turned off the car and got all my shit together before stepping out. When I looked over at the passenger seat, I noticed that Nariah was still knocked out. She was snoring loud as hell, but that didn't stop me from noticing her beauty. She truly looked like an angel. Everything about her was as natural as it could get, which is just what I had been searching for. I stepped out of the car and went around to get her out. When I opened the door, she raised her hand up and started mumbling.

"Where areeee, I work, and I sooooo wasted. My job….." she slurred.

I put one arm around her waist, then grabbed her legs and lifted her up. "Baby, don't worry about nothing. I got you."

I threw her arms around my neck and laid her head back on my chest. I knew she was gonna have to miss work tomorrow, but it wasn't shit I could do to prevent that. As fucked up as she was, she was gonna need all of the sleep she could get. I closed the door and locked her car, then headed inside of the house. As soon as I walked in, my alarm started sounding off.

"Fuck," I said as I rushed to the keypad with Nariah still in my arms.

I quickly entered the code, locked the door, and then went upstairs to the guest room. I placed Nariah on the bed, and took her heels off. This girl reeked of vomit, and I refused to let her sleep on my Frette Illusione sheets like that. She needed to get out of that dress a.s.a.p. I grabbed a white tee out of the drawer and a wet wash cloth out of the bathroom. I lifted her back and placed a pillow behind her.

"Noooo," she said as she laid there trying to wake up.

"I ain't trying to hurt you Nariah. I'm just trying to wipe you down and put this shirt on you, so you can sleep comfortably. Your dress is full of vomit, ma. You can't sleep with that shit on in my bed," I replied while unzipping the dress and sliding it off of her.

I pulled the white tee over her head, then passed the wash cloth around her mouth and chest. I wanted to clean her whole face, but I wasn't really trying to fuck with no makeup. She could do that shit in the morning. I picked up her dress and wiped it down as much as I could before placing it on the dresser. The shit still smelled, but not as much as it did before.

I walked around to the nightstand and placed her phone and keys in the drawer. I glanced over at her one more time to make sure she was straight, and she was. I walked out of the room and softly closed the door, then ran downstairs and sat on the sofa. I needed to call Allyson and run it with her before she came back here with all of her crazy shit. I wasn't in the mood to wrestle with her ass, and I damn sure as hell wasn't trying to disturb Nariah.

Before I could dial Allyson's number, my phone started vibrating; it was her. I wondered what Lexi's dumb ass told her, cuz she never called me unless I sent her a text and told her to. I answered the phone and just listened to feel her out.

"DERON!" she screamed into the phone.

I put my hand on my forehead and leaned forward. "Aye man, chill the fuck out. I ain't with that attitude shit tonight. Did Lexi give you my keys?"

"YEA, SHE DID. WHAT THE FUCK YOU GOT GOING ON DERON? WHAT BITCH YOU GOT OVER THERE? AND DON'T LIE NIGGA, CUZ LEXI TOLD ME AND EVERYBODY SAW YO ASS LEAVE WITH HER," she replied.

I knew she would be on some fuck shit. She knew how much I hated when she acted like we were still together. It's like she forgot about the agreement we made or something.

"Look bruh, don't come at me with that stupid shit. Whatever the fuck I got going on, ain't got shit to do with you or any of them messy hoes in that club. We got business to handle, and you sitting there worried about shit that's irrelevant to the fucking situation," I stated.

"I DON'T GIVE A FUCK ABOUT YOUR BUSINESS! DON'T BE BRINGING NO BITCH WHERE I MAKE MY FUCKING MONEY! DO YOU SEE ME BRINGING OTHER NIGGAS TO YOUR GAMES? THE FUCK YOU MEAN MY NIGGA! YOU FORGOT WHO THE FUCK I AM?!" she continued to scream.

I really wasn't in the mood to argue with this inbred ass bitch. She already knew what was up, but apparently she needed to be reminded.

"Say, look, I ain't about to keep going back and forth with you about no dumb shit. You work in a strip club, and pop your pussy for any nigga with a dollar. Ya feel me? And quit acting like we together my nigga. We just business partners, and you know that. So ain't no limits to who I can bring there or to my crib. If I wanna bring yo mama in this bitch I can. So calm yo fucking ass down, and chill the fuck out before I get your ass banned from all of my fucking games," I responded.

She knew what time it was when I mentioned her mom. See, Allyson was from the 5th Ward. When she started dancing, she didn't tell her people shit. She was making all of this money and blowing it, and had them believing she was working at Wal-Mart. Not once did she try to move her people in a nicer area or even move out of my fucking crib. Every time they asked her to come back home, she gave them a bum ass story about having to quit her job and starting over. So if her secret ever got exposed, shit would hit the fan.

Allyson took a deep breath. "What do you want to discuss Deron? I got the drop off from Nick, and I got your car keys. Everything is in duffel bags and in the trunk, and Kayla is gonna drive my car. She already called her dude and told him she had a play tonight. So what else do you wanna talk about? I'm not trying to go there with you. I know we have an agreement, and I'm not trying to mess that up. Just quit disrespecting me."

"Nobody is disrespecting you. You're disrespecting yourself by acting stupid. Now before you and Kayla get here acting all crazy and shit, I just want you to know that I do have company staying over until the morning," I replied.

"HOLD ON! WHAT COMPANY? I KNOW YOU AIN'T BRING THAT BITCH OVER THERE! I'M ON MY FUCKING WAY HOE! I GOT YOUR COMPANY! THAT BITCH BETTER BE GONE WHEN I PULL UP!" she yelled before hanging up.

"ALLYSON!" I screamed into the phone.

This bitch was really trippin. I tried to call her back, but as I expected, she sent me to voicemail. I already knew what was about to go down. I ran upstairs to check on Nariah and she was still sound asleep, so I decided to hop in the shower before bird brain pulled up. I needed to sober up as fast as I could in order to fully handle her ass.

*****

When I got out of the shower, I threw on some black Polo boxers, red Nike basketball shorts, and a black tee. I wanted to be as comfortable as I could be in case I had to wrestle with Allyson's ass. Sometimes she got out of control, and I had to slap her up to get her mind right. I hated having to do that, but that's just how far she'd take shit. I slid into my red and black Nike slippers, courtesy of the company, and made my way back downstairs. I had just signed an endorsement deal with them, so the merchandise was flowing in.

By the time I made it back downstairs, Allyson and Kayla were already outside. I had a mind to go out there and stop their asses at the door, but I wasn't tryna cause a scene. It was too early in the morning for that bullshit, and I didn't need HPD showing up at my crib. I sat on the sofa and turned on the t.v. A few seconds later, Allyson and Kayla walked in.

Allyson threw her purse down and ran around the coffee table. "OH, YOU WATCHING T.V., HUH NIGGA? WHERE THE BITCH AT?"

Here we go.

"Say bruh, calm that fucking shit down my nigga. You walking in here sounding stupid as fuck. Chill the fuck out Allyson," I replied while standing up.

"FUCK YOU! YOU CHILL THE FUCK OUT! YOU BRINGING BITCHES TO MY JOB AND SHIT WHILE I'M TRYING TO HANDLE BUSINESS FOR YOU! THEN YOU WANNA TELL ME YOU GOT COMPANY LIKE I'M SUPPOSED TO JUST BE OK WITH THAT! YOU MUST THINK I'M A GREEN BITCH, HUH? LIKE YOU CAN JUST DISRESPECT ME AND DO WHATEVER TO ME, AND I'MA JUST LET THAT SHIT FLY! YOU GOT ME FUCKED UP DERON! WHERE THAT BITCH AT? SHE BETTER NOT BE IN MY FUCKING BED! IS SHE IN MY FUCKING BED DERON, HUH?" she continued.

She turned around and moved in the direction of the stairs. I ran in front of her and blocked her from going up.

"Calm down and chill the fuck out son! You acting stupid my nigga! If you keep this shit up, you gon get the fuck out and go back to your fucking mama! I ain't got time for this shit! I pay these fucking bills Allyson! This my shit! I let YOU stay here! Remember? Quit letting that fucking powder get the best of you! This ain't the time or the place for all that!" I replied.

She pushed me in my face and tried to go around me. When she realized she couldn't, she stood in front of me and started yelling again.

"FUCK YOU DERON! I DON'T NEED YOU OR THIS FUCKING HOUSE! YOU NEED ME BITCH! I CAN GO BACK TO MY MAMA'S WITH NO PROBLEM! BUT THEN WHAT? WHO'S GONNA DO THE SHIT THAT I DO? WHO'S GONNA PUT THEIR LIFE AT RISK EVERY FUCKING NIGHT FOR YOU? YOU KEEP FORGETTING WHO NEEDS WHO! DON'T TRY TO CLOWN ON ME IN FRONT OF MY GIRL, CUZ SHE ALREADY KNOW THE REAL! YOU CAN TRY TO MAKE YOURSELF SEEM ALL BIG AND MIGHTY IF YOU WANT TO FOR THAT BITCH UPSTAIRS, BUT YOU AIN'T FOOLING NOBODY! EVERYTHING YOU GOT IS BECAUSE OF ME! NONE OF THAT SHIT CAME FROM YOUR LIL BASKETBALL GAMES! BUT SINCE YOU WANNA THREATEN ME, DON'T FORGET THAT I CAN EASILY GO TO THE BLOGS AND SHIT ON YOUR ENTIRE CAREER! THE ONLY BALLS YOUR ASS WILL EVER BOUNCE AGAIN WILL BE YOUR OWN! IS THAT WHAT THE FUCK YOU WANT?"

This bitch looked real childish standing there screaming and clapping her hands like a toddler. She thought she was making a point, but all she was really doing was digging her own grave and making my head hurt. I looked over at Kayla to see if she was buying this and the poor girl was still standing against the door holding the duffel bags. The look on her face spoke volumes, and I could tell she was scared as hell. I guess she wasn't used to seeing shawty act like this, but for me this was nothing.

I shifted my focus back to Allyson who was still screaming and throwing up gang signs. The more she ran her mouth, the more my head started to hurt. There was only one way to shut her crazy ass up. I grabbed her by her arm and started pulling her down the hallway.

"LET ME GO DERON," She screamed as she clawed at my hand.

I ignored her and continued to pull her until I made it to the bathroom. I opened the door and turned the light on, then grabbed her by the back of her neck and threw her inside. I walked in behind her and closed and locked the door. She punched me in my chest, then started trying to get to the doorknob. I grabbed her hands and held her still.

"Chill the fuck out Allyson, before you make my neighbors call the laws."

"FUCK YOU AND YOUR NEIGHBORS BITCH! LET ME OUT OF THIS FUCKING BATHROOM!" she screamed in my face as she squirmed and kicked.

"So it's fuck me?" I asked while looking into her eyes.

I wasn't trying to go there with Allyson, but I needed to stay on her good side in order to keep my business going at the club. I leaned in and kissed her on her neck. She pulled away and continued to scream.

"DON'T FUCKING TOUCH ME! LET ME OUT OF THIS FUCKING BATHROOM! KAYLA! GET A KNIFE AND COME OPEN THIS FUCKING DOOR!"

I looked at her and shook my head. "So this how we gonna end things?"

She turned to the right and looked at her reflection in the mirror, then teared up. "Deron, I'm tired of you playing with me like I'm just a hoe. You don't give a fuck about me, and I get it now. So just open the door and let me go about my business. You have your new bitch upstairs. You gon' be aight."

I grinned and let her hands go, then began unbuttoning her jeans. She cried and tried to move my hands out of the way.

"Stop Deron."

I ignored her and slid her jeans and thong down, then slid down my basketball shorts and boxers. She looked at my hard dick, then turned her head. I lifted her up by her legs, and slid her down on it, then backed her up into the wall. She closed her eyes, wrapped her arms around my neck, and then dropped her head forward. I used one hand to lift up her shirt and bra and sucked on her breasts as she moaned in my ear.

"Mmmmmmmmmm."

I thrusted my dick further inside of her, then grabbed her waist, and started bouncing her up and down. Allyson's pussy was wet as fuck. She clinched my dick with her muscles and dug her nails into my back, which caused me to bounce her faster. I watched her breasts bounce up and down as I drilled my dick inside of her.

"Aaaaahhhh, shit Deron. Fuckkkkk!" she cried out.

I needed to hurry up and make her nut before she woke up Nariah, so I grabbed her by her throat and turned her around while still holding her in the air. I wrapped my arm around her torso and pulled her close to me still holding her throat. I thrusted my dick into her as hard as I could and stroked her. Her legs immediately began to shake and her head fell into the wall.

"Deronnnnnn, I'm….. aaahahhhhhh."

I let go of her throat, then grabbed her by her waist and kept stroking her as fast as I could. She reached behind me and grabbed my shirt, then began moving her hips in a circle as she nut on my dick.

"Ahhhhhh, mmmmmm."

I looked down and watched as my dick went in and out of her while she nutted. The sight of Allyson's cum on my dick and the sounds she was making had my shit throbbing. A few seconds later, I felt myself about to nut. I pushed her head down and began drilling her shit again.

"Shit. I'm 'bout to bust," I said as I breathed hard into her neck.

I stroked her one last time and squeezed her ass while I shot my nut deep inside of her.

"Damn girl," I moaned as my body quivered.

I grabbed her breasts one last time, then slid my dick out of her, and let her down. She turned and slid down the wall, then looked up at me grinning. I laughed and pulled up my boxers and basketball shorts.

"You straight now?" I asked breathing hard.

She rolled her eyes and stood up, then pulled up her thong and jeans.

"You just showed me what I really mean to you."

I looked at her and frowned. "What the fuck are you talking about, bruh?"

"You just fucked me in your downstairs bathroom, while your new bitch was sleeping upstairs. You don't give a fuck about me or any of the shit that I've ever done for you. So FUCK YOU DERON!" she replied while buttoning her jeans.

I cocked my neck to the side and stood against the bathroom door. I had just given this girl the ride of her life and she was still on the same fuck shit. She had me fucked up if she thought I was about to kiss her ass. Yea she helped me handle my business and shit, but what one bitch won't do the next bitch will. I rubbed my hands together and looked at her as she patted her hair down in the mirror.

"Look Allyson, I have thanked you in more ways than one for what you do and have done for me. But what you've done will never amount to all the shit I done did for you. So if you wanna go, you can go my nigga. I'm not gonna fucking beg you stay where you don't wanna be. Just fucking go."

I snatched my keys out of her back pocket and opened the bathroom door. I walked out and walked up to Kayla, who was now sitting on the stairs, and grabbled the duffel bags out of her hand. She stood up and flinched, then walked past me and stood against the wall.

"Ain't nobody gonna touch you girl," I said while unlocking and opening the front door.

Next thing you know, Allyson's ass flew around the corner and slammed the door. She rolled her eyes and got right back in my fucking face.

"SO NOW YOU'RE KICKING ME OUT? REALLY! AFTER EVERYTHING WE DONE BEEN THROUGH? I GOTTA GO CUZ I'M TELLING YOU THE REAL. IS THAT WHAT YOU JUST SAID TO ME MY NIGGA? CUZ I DON'T THINK I HEARD RIGHT THE FIRST TIME!"

"Allyson just leave. You said what the fuck you had to say in the bathroom, so I really ain't tryna hear nothing else. Just take your purse and your home girl and bounce. I got shit to do," I replied as I went around her and stood in front of the stairs.

"FUCK YOU DERON! FUCK YOU AND THAT BITCH YOU GOT UPSTAIRS! I HOPE THAT HOE USE YOU FOR EVERYTHING YOU HAVE, AND I HOPE YOUR ASS END UP IN JAIL, BITCH! I'LL BE CALLING MEDIATAKEOUT AND TMZ TOMORROW MORNING TO TELL THEM ALL ABOUT YOUR LIL SIDE HUSTLE! MARK MY WORDS!" She screamed as she picked up her purse.

"You hope I end up where?" I asked while putting the duffel bags down.

"YOU HEARD ME NIGGA! I HOPE YOU END UP IN JAIL, BITCH! FOR LIFE, AND I HOPE YOUR HOE ASS LOSE EVERYTHING!" she continued to yell.

Now this bitch was going too far. She already knew how I felt about jail, so for her to stand there and wish that shit upon me was the ultimate disrespect. I grabbed Allyson by her neck and pushed her back. I wasn't gonna hit the bitch, but she was gonna think twice about crossing me again.

"DERONNNN, STOP! I CAN'T FUCKING BREATHE! STOP, PLEASE! I'M SORRY," she cried out as I squeezed my hand around her neck.

I continued to push her back. "Open the door Kayla!"

Kayla quickly turned around and opened the front door. Allyson was still scratching at my hand trying to get me to release my grip, so as soon as it was open I threw her neck back and let her go. Kayla looked at me with tears in her eyes and ran out. I shut the door behind her and locked it. I didn't want this to happen in front of her, but she could thank Allyson for that.

"NOW MOVE THE FUCK AROUND BEFORE SHIT GETS REAL!" I yelled from behind the door while setting the alarm.

I could still hear Allyson screaming and beating on her hood. "YOU WILL PAY FOR THIS BITCH! I

SWEAR YOU WILL! ON MY MAMA, YOU WILL PAY FOR THIS! WATCH YOUR FUCKING BACK DERON!"

A few seconds later I heard her car start. I looked out the window just in time to see her pulling off.

"Thank God," I said to myself.

By the way shit ended, I knew that this wouldn't be my last encounter with Allyson. Honestly though, I didn't give a fuck. I had my work and my bread, and the bitch was finally out of my house. That alone was enough to put a smile on my face.

I picked up the duffel bags and went back upstairs to check on Nariah. I wanted to make sure that all of the shit that had just taken place hadn't disturbed her. I stopped at the guest room, and cracked the door open. She was still in the same place I had left her. I was surprised that all of the noise hadn't woken her up, but extremely thankful that it didn't. There was no way I would have been able to easily explain any of this shit to her, had she woken up and came downstairs.

I closed the door, and headed to my room. It was now exactly 4 am. I knew that I was gonna be tired as fuck at practice, so I decided to just shoot my coach a text and let him know that I wouldn't be able to make it. After all the shit that had went down tonight I needed to rest, so I was willing to deal with any penalties that I might face like a man.

CHAPTER THREE – Nariah

Last night was all a blur to me. No matter how hard I tried to think, I couldn't remember anything. I definitely didn't know where the hell I was, or even how I ended up here. But what I did remember was that my ass had to be at STYLECIRCLE for 8 am. I looked over at the clock that was on the nightstand, only to see that it was 10:58 am. I was fucked.

I jumped out of the bed. "OH MY GOD!"

I frantically began searching for my things, when Deron suddenly rushed through the door.

"Nariah, you aight, ma?" he asked looking worried.

"No, I'm not alright. I'm late for work, I can't find my phone, and I just need to go. I don't know how I ended up here with you, but I need to leave now. Where are my things?" I angrily replied.

"Your keys and your phone are in the top drawer of the nightstand, and your dress is laid out on the dresser. Look Nariah, nothing happened last night. You had a lil too much to drink, so instead of letting you drive home I just brought you here," he explained.

I took off the shirt I had on and grabbed my dress off of the dresser. "You gave me too much to drink after I told you I had to go to work early. I asked you not to do that, and you did it anyway. Now I am late and most likely out of a job, so thank you Deron."

He sat on the bed with a disgusted look on his face. "Wait, so this is my fault? Nariah, by the time I got back to you, you had already finished the bottle. I ain't make you drink nothing, so don't try to pin this all on me. You're a grown ass woman. I'm not responsible for your actions."

I wasn't in the mood to argue about who was at fault. I needed to get my ass to work as soon as possible. As I was about to slip into my dress, I noticed that it smelled like vomit. There was no way that I could put it on and show up to my job like that. I threw the dress on the floor, and sat on side of the bed.

"My life is over," I said as I buried my face into my hands.

Deron stood up and walked over to the closet. He turned on the light and began rummaging through the hangers. "Look, I have something you can put on to make it to work."

I looked over my shoulder and rolled my eyes. "I'm not putting on anything that belongs to Allyson."

He looked at me and shook his head. Little did he know, I had heard everything that took place last night. When the bitch came in with all of that hollering and screaming it was hard for me to keep sleeping. Her voice irritated my soul, but I was really waiting on her to bust through the room. I didn't have the strength to go downstairs and intervene between the two of them, but I wasn't about to let her slide in here and catch me slipping. Deron walked out of the closet with a frosted metallic Neiman Marcus pencil skirt and a liquid satin cap-sleeve top to match. He threw the clothes on the bed and stood there with his hands in his pockets.

"This ain't Allyson's. This belonged to my sister."

I looked at him, then grabbed the clothes from off of the bed. I found it funny that he didn't question how I knew about Allyson, but I guess it didn't take much for him to realize that I was awake during their argument. I went into the bathroom to change and freshen up. I didn't have time to shower, so I just washed myself off as best as I could. I brushed my teeth with a towel, rinsed my face, and threw my hair back in a messy bun. I was a little upset that I didn't have my makeup, but truth be told, I didn't really need it. Besides, my appearance was the furthest thing from my mind. All I was worried about was the kind of mood my boss would be in when I finally arrived. I could only hope and pray that he'd be understanding of me being three hours late. I walked out of the bathroom and back into the room to get my things. Deron was still standing against in the middle of the floor watching me.

As I was walking out of the room, he grabbed my hand. "Nariah, please just hear me out. Just give me a minute to explain."

I pulled my hand away from him with my back still turned towards him. "Deron, I don't have a minute right now. Do you see what time it is? There's nothing to explain."

"Can you at least come back when you're done? I really need to talk to you," he said.

I turned and looked at him one last time before exiting the room.

"Maybe," I said as I walked out.

I briskly made my way downstairs and ran to my car. Good thing downtown wasn't too far away from here, cuz I would have really been fucked. I started my car and backed out of the driveway. While backing out, I noticed that Deron's car was all scratched up. I guess Allyson felt the need to key his shit before she left. Oh well, that was between them. As long as she hadn't touched my shit, I was good. I hated when a bitch when after the female instead of her nigga.

After finally finding my way out of that big ass subdivision, I got on the highway and rushed to my job. I needed something to wake me up. I didn't have time to stop for coffee, so I turned to the next best thing that would give me the boost I needed... trap music. I turned the radio on and went to the only station that I listened to when I didn't have my phone plugged in, KBXX 97.9 The Box. Right when I turned up the volume, my girl Cardi B's new song, Bodak Yellow rang out. It was exactly what I needed to jump start this fucked up morning I was having. I turned the volume up louder and pushed down on the accelerator. Cardi was giving me life. Fifteen minutes later, I made it to my job. I pulled into the parking lot and found a spot that was close to the door. I reached for my bag in the backseat, only to see that it wasn't there.

"SHITTTTTTTTTTT!!!!!" I screamed as I punched the steering wheel.

No bag, meant no folders, and no folders meant zero prints. My ass was just as good as dead. I turned the car off and grabbed my phone out of the cup holder. I knew I wouldn't be able to leave and go get my bag, so I was just gonna have to wing it. I got out of my car and ran into the building. I didn't even bother checking in with the receptionist. I flew to the elevator, but it was just my luck that the bitch was out of service.

"REALLYYYYYY!!!" I yelled out.

I went around to the opposite side of the hallway and began climbing the stairs. I hated taking the stairs in heels, but this was my only other option. I wasn't trippin though. I needed the exercise. Those lunch trips to Pappadeaux's were starting to do a number on my thighs. I made it to the 3rd floor and took a deep breath. I was nervous as hell, but all I could do at that point was face whatever would be thrown my way.

I walked into the studio and all eyes were on me. I had a mind to turn around and walk back out, but that would only make things worse. I found a chair at the back of the room and sat down. There were local investors seated all around me, and of course, my boss was standing right in the center of the floor pitching a Fall fashion idea to them. I was hoping he wouldn't say anything to me until the end, but when he saw my face he stopped mid-sentence.

"Ladies and gentlemen, could you excuse me for a couple of minutes please? I need to have a word with this beautiful young lady who just walked in. There are refreshments and doughnuts in the back that you are more than welcome to help yourselves to. I will only be a couple of minutes," my boss stated while giving a fake smile.

The investors stood up looking confused, and shifted their focus back to me. Their glares and stares made me feel very uncomfortable. I was embarrassed as fuck, and I knew that shit was about to hit the fan. My boss walked over to me with a stern look on his face. Before he could say anything, I stopped him and started explaining.

"I am so sorry Florence. I had a horrible night last night, and I completely lost track of the time. I promise it will never happen again," I explained.

"Nariah, you have brought so many wonderful ideas to this company. But one thing you have never done is showed up empty handed to an extremely important meeting like you are doing today. For the past few weeks, you have been late a total of eight times. Eight times Nariah! I do not know what has gotten into you my dear, or what you have gotten yourself into. And quite frankly, I honestly do not care. Unfortunately, we will not be needing your services today or any day after for that matter. You are dismissed." He replied.

I crossed my arms and looked at him in awe. "You're firing me? Like are you seriously doing this right now?"

Florence looked me up and down then pushed his glasses up on his nose. "I prefer the word terminating."

I could not believe this shit. This little Rumpelstiltskin looking bitch was really letting me go after all of the blood, sweat, and tears that I put into this company. I stayed up countless nights going over prints and graphics just to make sure his ass was covered. I dealt with stuck up ass wanna be models on the daily just so he wouldn't have to and here he was "terminating" me in front of a group of investors. Oh hell no. He had the game fucked up.

"Let me tell you something Florence. I have worked my ass off and bent over backwards for you since day one. For years, I have put my own brand on the line by working beside your trifling ass and this is how you repay me? Did you forget who stood by you during all of your scandals and lawsuits? I had to put my own shit aside to cover your ass and help you secure your fucking spot in this industry. Do you know how hard it was to help you win and watch you take credit for my shit? If it weren't for me you wouldn't be half the designer you are today. You would still be selling studio time on Groupon bitch, but yet you're trying to fire me cuz I was late. So what if I was late. Who the fuck cares? I'm here now, and from the looks of it you need me. Your investors were sitting there as stiff as the wig on top of your head, like if they were at a funeral home listening to your ass pitch a deal on caskets. But you know what, FUCK YOU! I QUIT! I HOPE YOUR SHINY, SQUEAKY ASS GETS THE RIDE OF YOUR LIFE ONCE EVERYONE REALIZES THAT IT WAS ME WHO KEPT YOU IN THE LATEST FASHIONS!" I responded before walking away.

I refused to allow him to destroy me. He could fire me a million times. According to me and everyone else in the room, I had quit.

Florence stood there with his hands covering his mouth. "Excuse the pumpkin spice latte out of me?"

"Oh, and by the way," I continued while turning around and flipping my hair. "While you're standing there trying to make it seem like you're so high and mighty in front of these investors, make sure you tell them how the designs you're trying to pitch to them are MY prints that I designed. Since you're so bad and fucking bold, tell them that. A real designer doesn't have to put their name on someone else's prints. They create and come up with their own shit boo." I stated as I walked out and slammed the door.

I stood outside of the door for a few minutes to catch my breath. I hadn't gone off on anyone like this in a long time, but I knew that it would happen sooner or later. I had been holding too much in, and it was only a matter of time before I got it all off of my chest. I walked away from the door and pulled out my phone. I needed to text Deron and let his ass know what had just happened. This was all his fault, and he was going to have to do something about this.

When I made it back down to the first floor, I noticed that the receptionist was laughing. I didn't know what she was laughing at, but seeing as how she was always on my boss' dick I assumed that she was laughing at me. For some reason he always felt the need to tell her everything that went on in the studio. I hated that shit, and truth be told, I didn't really care for her either.

I strolled over to the desk and slammed my hand down on the bell that was sitting near the computer. "What the fuck are you laughing at hoe?"

She immediately stopped laughing and sat there looking confused.

"I don't know what the hell is so funny, other than the fact that your husband has been fucking Janessa from the 5th floor since the day she started working here. Every afternoon you can catch his dick up her ass in room 237 at the hotel across the street. You're always in everyone else's business, but I bet you didn't know that, huh? Of course you didn't. Now you can laugh bitch. Ha, ha, ha, you're welcome." I stated as I walked away and exited the building.

When I got to my car, I noticed that Deron had texted me back telling me to come over. He didn't have to tell me twice. I couldn't wait to get in that ass. I got in my car and started it, and headed back to his house. This nigga had some explaining to do, because not only was I now jobless, but my chances of getting hired anywhere else was ruined, at least in the fashion industry.

On the way to his crib, I stopped and picked me up a 4 for $4 from Wendy's. I wasn't really that hungry, but I needed something greasy to help settle my stomach after all of the liquor I had downed last night. I still felt a little weak, but I was more hurt than anything. I let the job that I had fought so hard for slip right out of my hands over a nigga I hadn't even slept with yet. The struggle was real.

*****

When I made it to Deron's house, my heart was racing. I had so much on my mind, and I didn't know how to think or even feel about everything that had just taken place in the last few hours. I parked my car on side of his and stepped out. I noticed that his car was now covered, so I assumed he had seen the scratches. It would've made more sense to cover it up before it got scratched, but whatever. That wasn't my issue.

I rang the doorbell and knocked on the door. I wanted to make sure he knew that I was out here before Allyson's crazy ass decided to pop out of the bushes or something. I wasn't afraid of her, but I wasn't trying to get into no shit either. I was already dealing with enough, and the last thing I needed was to get attacked by some stripper bitch gone mad.

When Deron finally opened the door, my mouth dropped. He was standing there in nothing but a towel. I didn't want to get sidetracked and forget why I was here, so I stared straight ahead and marched right past him. But believe me when I tell you, he was looking good as hell. He still had water dripping down his body, his goatee was glistening, and his dick was looking like the eggplant emoji behind that towel. He looked GOOD!

"Get it together Riah," I whispered to myself as he closed the door behind me.

I sat on the sofa and crossed my legs. It was hard not to get wet for this nigga, especially since I hadn't had sex in over a year. But that's not why I was here.

Deron locked the door and stood against the wall. "How'd it go?"

"Not good. Not good at all," I replied while pretending to look at my phone.

I didn't want to keep staring at him, so I needed to keep myself distracted.

"You aight?" He asked as he walked over to me.

I couldn't let this nigga get close to me, so I stood up and walked in the opposite direction. "Actually, no I'm not. I got fired today. I ended up cussing my boss and his ex out before I left, so my career is basically over."

"You cussed his ex out?" he asked looking confused.

"Yea, she's the receptionist. Apparently after he fired me he sent her a memo about it. When I was leaving she was sitting there laughing, so I cussed her ass out and let her know about her husband's affair. I feel horrible now though, because I should've never went about it that way. That's not who I am," I explained.

Deron walked around to where I was and grabbed my hands. "Relax Nariah. Everything will be ok. It's just a job. You could always get another one."

Wow, just a job. This was not just a job. This was my career that we were talking about. No matter how he tried to spin things, it was still his fault that I got fired. I pulled my hands away from him and pushed him.

"You don't get it do you? Just a job! I could always get another one! Do you hear yourself right now? This was my career Deron. Just like basketball is your career, fashion is mine. I can't just walk into a studio and get another job. It doesn't work that way. Unlike you, I have to work for what I want. Shit don't just fall from the sky for me. I have to open my own doors and pave my own way. There's no red carpet laid out for Nariah. So no, it's NOT just a job."

I walked away from Deron and sat back on the sofa.

"Hold up ma. How you figure shit is just handed to me?" he asked. "Nothing gets handed to me. I gotta work for my shit just like you do. That's what's wrong with the world today. Everybody thinks athletes got it good; like because we play ball, we're exempt from dealing with life. We go through the same shit that someone who works a 9-5 goes through. We can get fired, just like we can lose endorsements. We don't get no kind of special treatment. If anything, they ride our ass 10 times harder cuz of all those damn bets and shit. If you expect me to feel sorry for you after the shit you just said, guess what, I don't. Cuz just like you got fired for showing up late to work today, I got benched for missing practice this morning. I was too fucking tired to go run up and down the court after babying your drunk ass last night."

Oh hell no. I know this nigga was not blaming me for missing practice. If it wasn't for his ass getting me drunk, he wouldn't have had to miss practice. He had me fucked up.

"Deron first off, all of this is YOUR fault, whether you want to admit it or not. You were the one who kept pumping me with alcohol, even AFTER I asked you not to. So don't sit here and try to put this shit on me. You wouldn't have had to baby me if you wouldn't have been so fucking persistent about me drinking. And as far as you being too fucking tired, that definitely has nothing to do with me. Maybe you should think back to the argument between you and Allyson last night. That's why the fuck you're tired. I heard everything that went on between the two of you, and the shit lasted awhile. So take your fucking charge and stop acting like a spoiled brat," I responded.

Deron looked at me and laughed. I guess he was shocked at the way I was coming at him, but I was never the type to bite my tongue. There was no way that I was about to let him talk to me that way, especially when he was the one in the wrong.

"Take my charge? This is coming from a grown ass woman who don't even remember killing a bottle of champagne last night. Look, we can sit here and point fingers at each other all day, but that won't solve shit. If you feel like it's my fault that you lost your job, then fine I'm sorry that you lost your job. But this shit that we're doing right now ain't cool. I put Allyson out for the exact same thing last night, and I would hate to have to do the same to you," he replied.

I know this nigga was not comparing me to Allyson. He had a lot of nerve.

I stood up and walked towards the door. "You know what? Since all of this is funny to you and you don't understand what you have done, I'll put myself out. You can keep your shitty apology and shove it up your ass."

I unlocked the door and walked out leaving Deron standing there speechless. I didn't expect him to run behind me, and I honestly didn't want him to. His attitude was fucked up, and he obviously had no remorse for all of the shit he had just caused me. Then for him to compare me to a stripper! He must have lost his rabbit ass mind. I was nothing like Allyson, and she was nowhere near the level that I was on.

As soon as I got in my car and started it, the tears started falling. In less than 24-hours, I had let a complete stranger come into my life and turn it upside down; my heart was shattered. I should've never went to that club last night. But more important, I should've never stopped and talked to this nigga when he tried to get my attention. Had I known that all of this would have transpired, I would have just got in my car and called for security to make him leave the premises. I don't know what I was going to do, but I had to think of something. Rent was coming around, and my savings were almost depleted. I must confess, this was a lesson well learned.

Chapter Four – Deron

I knew that I was wrong for coming at Nariah the way that I did, but she needed to hear the truth. Yea, I offered her a drink, but she still chose to drink it. If she knew that she couldn't handle her liquor the adult thing to do would have been to place the glass down and leave it there, not down an entire bottle of champagne in less than thirty minutes. I felt bad about her losing her job, but she rubbed me the wrong way when she started talking out the side of her neck. Nariah didn't know shit about what I went through as an athlete, and she damn sure didn't know anything about my life. The way she judged me was fucked up, and that's what made me compare her to Allyson.

Speaking of Allyson, she had been calling me since early this morning and was now calling again. I know she probably wanted to discuss what happened last night, but talking to her was the furthest thing from my mind. When I told her to leave I meant that shit, so I wasn't trying to listen to her beg to come back.

After Nariah left, I went upstairs to finish getting dressed. I had a meeting with Kenton, a plug I had met after one of my games, to get this weight off of my hands and I only had an hour before it was time to pull up. I didn't wanna look like the bad boy that I usually looked like, so I decided to dress a lil more casual. I threw on a white Eric Dress floral print vogue blazer, a pair of black slacks, and a pair of matching white Will perforated penny drivers. I topped everything off with a few sprays of Polo Black.

I walked out of the room and hit up the plug to let him know that I was on my way. Instead of answering the phone, he sent a text confirming everything. We were meeting up at this Chinese restaurant in the West Chase district away from all of the cameras. I picked up my Ray Bans off of the coffee table and put them on. I grabbed my keys, set the alarm, and headed out of the front door.

I walked out of the house at 3:11 pm. I was making good timing. I uncovered my car and put the car cover in the trunk. Last night, Allyson's bitch ass keyed the fuck out of my driver's side door. I guess that was her way of getting back at me for kicking her out, but I wasn't trippin. I had already made an appointment with the dealership for another paint job. If I flashed out every time a bitch keyed my car, I'd be in a mental institution somewhere. These hoes out here were real disrespectful at times, and for some reason they felt like keying a nigga shit was the only way to prove a point.

I started my car and backed out of the driveway. My neighbors were outside looking as always, so I decided to blast my music on their asses. I plugged up my phone and went to my music. I only jammed two real niggas in this car which were Future and Yo Gotti. I clicked on my Future playlist and cranked the volume all the way up. I put my windows down and smashed on the gas.

Living next door to the Peterson's was like living in a nightmare. Mr. Peterson was a doctor and his wife was a lawyer, so they were very conservative people. They didn't have any kids, and they didn't really care for people like me. By people like me, I mean athletes. Aside from me, there were a few other athletes who lived on the block. They were always throwing parties and making noise, which was part of the reason why my neighbors hated me. The main reason though, was because Mr. Peterson caught his wife drooling over me one day when I was outside with my boys. In his eyes, she was cheating on him with me. Ever since then, nothing was the same.

I quickly turned off my street before they tried to call the laws on me. I hopped on the tollway and almost had to come to a complete stop. Traffic was backed up due to a car accident, but I wasn't about to let that stop me from getting to where I needed to be. Growing up in Houston, I knew exactly how to maneuver in this shit. I put on my emergency flashers and started boss hogging through traffic. When I finally got to a clear path, I started doing 80 in a 65. I wasn't trying to catch a ticket, but money was waiting on me and I had to get there fast by any means necessary. I got to the restaurant and only had ten minutes to make my way inside and find out where this nigga was sitting.

I hopped out of my whip and locked the doors. I already had the duffel bags in the trunk in case the deal went as planned, so I needed to make sure everything was secured. I walked into the restaurant and went straight into the dining area. The host looked at me like she had a problem. Apparently she didn't know who I was, but that was a good thing. I wasn't trying to sign no autographs or take pictures at a time like this. I was here for one thing and one thing only and that was business. I walked around the dining area for a few seconds until I found the big homie.

When I spotted where he was sitting, I took off my Ray Ban's and walked up to his booth. I looked over and noticed that he had a lil tender bitch with him, which to my surprise was Allyson. What the fuck was she doing here?

"Yo, what up fam?" I said while extending my arm out to shake his hand.

Allyson looked up and her eyes got big. I guess she was just as shocked as I was.

The guy stood up to shake my hand. "Deron, what's good star player?"

"Shit, trying to get like you," I laughed as we both sat down.

I looked over at Allyson while laughing. She was sitting there looking like she had just seen a ghost. I guess she was on a mission as well, which was fine with me. If she thought that I was here to throw dirt on her, she thought wrong. Even though she had just keyed the fuck out of my car less than 24-hours ago, I wouldn't do that to her. I wasn't the type to stop anybody from eating.

The guy rubbed Allyson's leg and handed me a menu. "Deron, I would like for you to meet my lovely wife Allyson."

I turned my head to the right and laughed. What the fuck? Did this nigga just say his wife? This hoe had a lot of explaining to do. She was just on my dick, and now all of a sudden she's married. I wonder if he knew that his wife was popping her pussy at the club every weekend.

I smiled and turned my attention to her, and extended my arm across the table to see if she would react. "Nice to meet you Allyson. I'm Deron."

She sat there with a cold-eyed vacant look and shook my hand. If looks could kill I would've been a dead man. Shawty was pissed.

"Nice to meet you Deron," she said as she quickly let go of my hand.

Kenton looked at her and then back at me. "I sense the two of you have met already met."

I put the menu down and laughed. "Oh, nah. This is my first time meeting her. Although, she does look like someone I've seen before."

Allyson sipped her drink and cleared her throat. "Well, you know what they say, everyone has a twin walking the Earth somewhere."

Damn, this bitch didn't even sound like the super thot that she usually sounded like. She was really sitting there getting her Young & the Restless on. I wanted to burst her bubble so bad, but I knew I had to keep it cool. I didn't wanna mess up what I had going on. She was gonna have to explain this shit later though. Make no mistake about it.

"Yea, you're right about that," I responded.

Kenton continued to rub her leg. "Allyson has been gone for the past eight months, and finally decided to come back home last night. Hopefully, she's done with the disappearing acts.

Allyson looked at me with a red face, then turned to Kenton. "Baby, do you mind if I excuse myself? I'm suddenly not feeling so well. I think it's this knock off filtered water I just drank. You know I'm not used to tap water."

"Maybe you need some milk," I said while looking down at the menu.

Allyson's ass was really trying to play that good wife role, but I saw right through that shit. Nothing was wrong with her. Her only issue was that she was getting caught up in her lies. I couldn't believe this bitch. Eight months ago is when she showed up to my crib with that bogus as story about her and her stepdad. I should've known that bitch was lying when she refused to let me go confront him.

Kenton glared at her with a confused look on his face. "Uh, yea baby, I guess. Go right ahead. I'll call you an Uber and meet you back at the house once we wrap things up," he replied.

Allyson leaned in and kissed him before getting up. She then turned her attention to me.

"Deron, it was nice meeting you. Good luck with your next game," she said before walking away.

"Thank you. I hope you feel better by tonight," I replied.

She rolled her eyes and turned away. She was a fool if she thought that I was just gonna take the shots she was throwing at me and not shoot any of my own. I was about to put her ass on front street, but I decided to save that for a later date. When Allyson left the booth, the waitress came over to take my order. I really wasn't hungry or thirsty, but to keep from being rude I just told her to bring me a Sprite and some egg rolls. I just wanted to seal the deal and get back home. Now that Allyson's fake ass was gone, it was time to talk numbers.

When the waitress left, Kenton folded his arms and looked at me. "So Deron, what you got for me my man?"

"I got nothing but the best, pure 90% Columbian cocaine. No additives and it has never been stepped on," I replied.

Kenton rubbed his chin. "Hmm, I see."

I leaned forward and pulled a small vial out of my back pocket.

"Here, I even brought a sample for you try out," I said while handing it to him.

Kenton took the vial and opened it. He tasted a bit of it first, then put some on the tip of his finger and sniffed. A couple of minutes went by, and he was leaned back into the booth as calm as ever.

"That's the best shit I've had in years," he stated.

I nodded my head and let out a chuckle. "Yo man, that's good to hear."

I had this nigga exactly where I wanted him. As high as he was right now, I knew he'd be willing to take the rest of this shit off of my hands. Kenton was the type of nigga that got high on his own supply. I could tell by how quick he reached for the vial. The nigga was a junkie on the cool, which is probably why he married Allyson's ass.

"How much more of that shit do you have?" Kenton asked.

When I was about to answer, the waitress came back with my order. She was smiling hard as hell, so I assumed she now knew who I was. When she placed everything down on the table, she stood with her hand on her hip and looked at me.

"Is there anything else that you would like on or off of the menu?" she flirtatiously asked.

I laughed and handed her a $100 bill. "Nah, we straight. But thank you for your assistance. Keep the change."

She reached for the money and slid me her number, then walked away. I placed it in my pocket and took a sip of my drink, then got right back to the business.

"Right now, I have a total of 12 keys," I replied.

Kenton sat up and pulled out his phone. "Marvelous. Would you like to make an offer? I want all of them."

My eyes opened wide. That is exactly what I wanted to hear.

"I can let it go for $360 G's," I said hoping he'd be ok with my price.

Kenton went to his calculator on his phone. He played around on it for a couple of seconds, then looked up with a devilish grin on his face.

"Deal. How soon can we exchange?" he asked.

"Shit, I got it on me now." I responded while pulling out my car keys.

Kenton took one last sip of his drink and stood up. "Well, let's get to it."

I stood up and followed Kenton out of the restaurant to his car. He was parked right next to me, which was perfect but suspect. He popped open his trunk and pulled out two duffel bags that looked similar to mine.

"Inside of each bag is $175k. You can either count it here in front of all of these people, or you can take my word for it and we can keep it moving," he stated.

I could tell that he was about his business, so I just took the bags and trusted his word. If anything was short, I knew where to find him.

I popped my trunk and threw them inside, then handed him mine.

"There are 6 keys in each bag bro. You can open it up and check them out for yourself."

Kenton placed the bags in his trunk, unzipped them, and started counting. When he was done counting, he zipped the bags back and closed his trunk.

"It was nice doing business with you Deron. If you need anything, you have my number. Feel free to give me a call," he said while walking back inside of the restaurant.

"Aight cool," I responded and got in my car.

I don't know what it was, but something didn't feel right about the way this nigga handled the last ten minutes of this deal. It's almost as if he was trying to set me up. The only thing that made me think otherwise was the fact that he couldn't pin nothing on me without getting himself caught up. I quickly started my car and burned out of the parking lot. I was now $350,000 richer and ready to celebrate. There was something that I had to do first though.

When I got to the light, I picked up my phone and sent Allyson a text. The stunt she pulled at the restaurant was weighing heavy on my mind. What I was really curious about was this marriage shit. If she could hide a whole husband, I wonder what else she could be hiding. When she texted me back, I told her to meet me at my crib. I didn't wanna discuss none of what happened over the phone. This called for a face to face discussion. She sent me a text back a few moments later declining my invitation. After the shit that had just went down, I could kinda understood why. I wouldn't want to meet up with someone I had been lying to for almost a year either.

I threw my phone on the seat and pulled off from the light. I didn't have any more words left for this hoe. She just better not let me see her again cuz shit wouldn't be as peachy as it was at the restaurant. The person I was worried about was Nariah. I hadn't heard from her since she left my crib earlier, and I was still feeling a lil bad about what had transpired between us. I wasn't ready to try and apologize again just yet though. Shit was still too fresh. What I needed to do was get in touch with my coach and see what was up. He sounded pretty pissed on the voicemail he left this morning. I was gonna make it a point to call him back when I got home.

When I was finished running the streets and handling a few errands, I finally made it back home a little after 8:00 pm. I was exhausted as fuck, and my head was still hurting. I was still lit about the exchange between me and Kenton, but once I got inside and got comfortable I changed my mind about going out. After the day I had, I just wasn't really feeling it.

I sat on the edge of my bed and stared into space. I couldn't stop thinking about Nariah. I tried to call her a few more times before I came back here to see if I could meet up with her, but her phone kept going straight to voicemail. Either she was ignoring my calls or she had her phone off. I don't think she would go as far as ignoring me, but I don't blame her if she was. I'd ignore me too after the things I said earlier.

I lied back on the bed for a minute and closed my eyes. My mind was racing with a million thoughts. I quickly popped back up when I thought about that voicemail from my coach earlier. I grabbed my phone and sent him a text to see if we could meet up tomorrow. Instead of texting back, he chose to call. I wasn't in the mood to deal no more bullshit, but I really didn't have a choice.

I made the sign of the cross before picking up the phone, then took a deep breath. I hadn't been much of a saint lately, but I needed all of the blessings I could get.

"What up coach?"

"You know you done fucked up right?" He asked angrily.

"Yea, but I just had a lot going on today. I ain't wanna go to practice with a bunch of shit on my chest and not be able to perform," I replied.

I couldn't go into detail without letting him know about my trip to the strip club last night, so I tried to keep it as short as possible. Strip clubs were off limits during the week of a game.

"What you had going on today doesn't pay your bills or mine, and it damn sure as hell doesn't secure your spot on the team. We have a game coming up, and everyone is ready except you," he said.

"Coach, it ain't nothing for me to get on the court and do what I do. You know this," I stated.

"What I know is that you're benched for this week's game, and if you miss practice one more time you'll be out for the rest of the season. I hope whatever you had going on today was worth it," he said before hanging up.

I jumped up off of the bed and threw my phone against the wall. I knew this shit was gonna happen. One of the biggest home games was only a few days away, and my dumb ass would be on the side line riding the bench.

Chapter Five - Nariah

My entire ride home was painful. All I wanted to do is crawl in my bed and sleep. I couldn't understand how I had let this happen, and even though I blamed a lot of it on Deron, some of it was my fault too. The more I thought about the situation at hand, the more I remembered how things played out last night. I don't recall downing a whole bottle of champagne, but for me to end up at Deron's house I had to have downed something. I didn't want to admit it earlier, but he was right about everything. I should've been more responsible.

When I got back home, I immediately jumped in the shower. It felt so good to just stand under the water there and let it run down my back. It helped relieve some of the stress that was weighing heavily on my shoulders. I grabbed my Shea Moisture Raw Shea Butter Body Wash and poured some on my washcloth. I scrubbed my body from top to bottom, then stood back under the water. Once all of the soap was off of me, I stepped out and wrapped myself in a towel. I wiped the steam off of the mirror and began combing out my hair. A couple of minutes later, my phone began to vibrate. I looked down at my screen, and just as I thought, it was Deron.

He had been calling off and on all day. I wanted to pick up my phone and answer it, but I didn't feel like arguing anymore. My head was still throbbing from all of the yelling and screaming I did earlier, so it was best if we let things die down before we spoke to each other again. I continued to run the comb through my hair and stare at my reflection. Looking in the mirror caused me to tear up. My life was now a mess, and the one person I needed the most, was no longer here and that person was my mother.

Despite everything that I went through with her, she was the only person that I could run to about any and everything. And right now, I needed her more than ever. When I was done combing and wrapping my hair, I dried myself off and went into my room. I slipped into one of my favorite silk gowns, then strolled over to my closet and pulled down a jewelry box from the top shelf. I opened it and took out the only piece I had left of my mother, her rosary. I walked back into the room and kneeled down on side of the bed. I placed my hands in front of me and put my head down.

"Mom, if you can hear my right now, I need you. I need you to help and guide me in the right direction. I'm lost without you ma. Nothing is the same since you've been gone. I don't have any friends. Laya hasn't come back. Life just isn't what I imagined it would be without you. It's ten times harder. I lost my job today and I'll probably end up losing this apartment. I'm losing myself ma." I took a deep breath and squeezed the rosary. "Your face crosses my mind daily. I hear your voice every morning, noon, and night but I can't reach you and it's killing me. I don't know what to do. I don't know where to turn. I just wish that you were here to tell me everything will be ok."

I sat against the bed and began to sob. I never truly realized how much I needed my mother until she was gone. Yes, she was a drug addict, but that didn't take away the fact that she was also my best friend, my confidant, and my protector. When I got taken away from her, it didn't hurt as bad because I knew that I'd eventually find my way back home. But when she died, I felt a pain that I had never felt before, because I never got a chance to say goodbye and the guilt of her death still lingers in my heart.

I got up off of the floor and climbed into bed. The tears were falling endlessly. I placed the rosary under my pillow and closed my eyes. I just needed to rest, and hopefully tomorrow would be a better day.

I woke up the next morning to 27 missed calls. Six were from a few of my former colleagues, and the rest were Facetime calls from Deron. I don't know what he could possibly have to say after the way he went off on me yesterday, but I was curious to find out. I got up out of the bed and went into the bathroom to brush my teeth and fix myself up. I couldn't talk to anyone with a dirty mouth or a tear stained face. When I was done with that, I put on my robe and sat on the bed to Facetime Deron.

When the video popped up, I noticed that he was still lying in bed shirtless. Gosh, he was fine. He sat up and looked into the screen. "Good morning. I didn't think you'd call back."

I let out a sigh before responding. "What do you want Deron?"

"Damn, no good morning? I just wanna let you know I'm sorry for the way I came at you. I shouldn't have flipped out the way I did. I just had a lot on mind and was still pissed about missing practice," he replied.

"I get that you were pissed about practice, but how do you think I felt. You still have your job. I don't," I said while looking off into the distance.

I didn't want him to see the pain in my eyes.

"Nariah, a job doesn't define you," he stated.

I looked into the screen with a confused look on my face. Here we go again.

"It may not define me, but it pays my bills. You know what Deron, I don't know why I even called. You still don't get it. You're saying you're sorry, but you still don't understand what you did wrong."

He scrunched up his face then put his arm behind his head. "What you mean I don't understand what I did wrong Nariah? I know what I did, and I apologized for it. I don't know no nigga who would keep trying to redeem himself to a female he barely knows like I've been doing. Stop trippin, your attitude is what got you where you are now. I'm starting to feel like I should've just left the shit alone."

I laughed and stared into the screen. Deron was totally out of line. Maybe I was a difficult female to please, but I know my worth and I expected to get treated a certain way. And the way he was acting right now just proved to me that he was incapable of meeting my expectations.

"You're not the only one who's starting to have regrets, cuz I swear I should've never given you the time of day. I knew what kind of nigga you was to begin with, but I still gave you the time of day. Good luck with your career

Deron, and have a nice life. I never want to hear from or see your disrespectful ass again."

His eyes got big, but before he could say anything else I ended the call. I was tired of the charades and bullshit. We hadn't known each other long enough for it to even be all of that. If this is who he was and how he treated women that he just met, then I could only imagine what it would be like to actually date him.

I went to my settings on my phone and blocked his number. Enough was enough.

Two Months Later

"Hello, may I speak to Nariah Wilson?" the woman on the phone asked.

"Yes, this is Nariah," I responded.

"Great. My name is Reagan Louvierre. I'm with the Department of Health and Human Services. I am calling about your SNAP application. Are you still in need of assistance, and if so, do you have a few minutes to spare for a phone interview to determine your eligibility for benefits?"

I know you're probably shocked, but yes. This was now my reality. As embarrassing as it was, I was forced to apply for food stamps. Losing my job really put me in a bind. Florence had completely destroyed my name in the fashion world, so no one wanted to even think about giving me an interview. I used my last check to pay my rent for three months, and the unemployment I was getting every week didn't do any justice. Once I finished paying all of my bills and buying toiletries, I was strapped. I could barely afford to buy two packs of meat, so I had to swallow my pride and do what was necessary.

I quickly sat up straight on the sofa. "Yes ma'am. I have time."

"Wonderful. Now before we begin, in order to create an accurate record of our conversation this call may be monitored or recorded for quality assurance purposes," the woman continued.

"Ok," I responded.

"We will begin with the basics first and move up from there. Nariah, can you tell me how many people are in living in the home?" the woman asked.

"Just me," I replied.

"Are you single, married, divorced, separated, or widowed?" she asked.

"I'm single."

"Do you have any kids?"

"No."

"Ok. Before I get to the next question, can you verify your date of birth and social security number for me please?"

I hated giving out personal information over the phone, but I knew that it was required. I gave her the information that she requested and waited for the next question. I didn't know that in order to be on government assistance you had to give away your entire life story. I was beginning to get annoyed.

"Thank you. Are you or anyone in the home pregnant?" the woman asked.

I took a deep breath and slapped my hand on my forehead. "No. I don't have kids and I don't want any, and I just told you that I live alone. I'm not even fucking anyone right now. It's just me; me, myself, and my toys that can't get me pregnant."

The woman paused and cleared her throat before asking the next question. I guess my response rubbed her the wrong way, but shit they wanted to know too fucking much.

"Are you currently employed?" the woman asked.

"No, I am not. If I was, I wouldn't be applying for food stamps," I responded.

There was a moment of silence before the woman said anything else.

"Miss Wilson, I understand that you may be bothered by the many questions that are being asked and I do apologize. However, I am just doing my job. If you would like me to stop and wrap up your case I can, but if you do not finish this interview you will not be eligible for benefits and will not be able to apply again for at least 6 months. The choice is yours."

I wasn't trying to have an attitude with her, but I was tired of answering so many damn questions. If these programs were put in place to help, then they should do just that. I shouldn't have to jump through hoops just to get assistance. I worked my ass off for years and paid hella taxes, so I didn't appreciate being interrogated like that. But she was right, she was only doing her job, and being in the position I was in, I had no choice but to accept it and just answer the stupid questions.

"I understand," I replied.

"Would you like to continue the interview?" the woman asked.

"Yes I would."

The woman read over a few more things, then began gathering information about my bills. I was also asked about my assets, bank account, and savings. By the end of the interview, she damn near knew everything about me except the date my period came every month.

"Miss Wilson, after reviewing your application and going over the answers from your interview it has been determined that you are indeed eligible for benefits. You will be awarded $187.00 on the 12th of every month for the next 6 months to purchase eligible food items at participating SNAP retailers. Eligible food items do not include hot food, fast food, beer, or alcohol and tobacco. When your 6 months are almost up, we will send out a renewal letter that will include various forms for you to fill out. You will also receive a list of any documents that we may need from you. If you do not turn in the forms and the requested documents in by the deadline, your benefits will expire, and you will have to apply again. Now, do you have a way to get to one of our offices to pick up your card?"

"Yes I do," I replied.

"Awesome. When you go to the office, make sure you bring your valid state issued ID or driver's license with you along with a piece of mail to verify your residential address. Once your case has been updated, you will be given a card that you may activate the same day. If you need help learning how to use your card or setting up your pin, you can ask the person at the window or you may dial the 1-800 number on the back of the card and do it yourself. Do you have any questions or concerns that you would like to go over before I end the call?" she continued.

"No ma'am."

"Ok, once again, my name is Reagan Louvierre. I hope you have a clear understanding of everything that we went over during this interview. I wish you lots of luck on your job search, and I hope you have a wonderful day. Good bye," She said before ending the call.

I hung up the phone and let out a huge sigh of relief. For a minute, I thought my mouth was gonna get me denied. I ran upstairs and got dressed, then headed to the office to pick up my card. After I finished finalizing everything at the office, I got in my car and went to Wal-Mart. I didn't have anything in my refrigerator or in the freezer, and my cabinets were just as empty.

I found a spot at Wal-Mart and briskly walked into the store. I was a little nervous about shopping with food stamps, but happy as hell at the same time. I grabbed a basket and pulled up my grocery list on my phone.

"Wow," I said to myself as I scrolled through my list. I needed a lot more than I thought, but with only $187.00 to spend I had to shop wisely.

I zipped through the store and got what I needed, then headed to the checkout. All of the lines were long, so I just got in one that was closest to the door. I stood in line and started reading an article on my phone. Suddenly, I felt a tap on my shoulder. I turned around to see who it was and almost screamed. Just as I assumed, it was Deron. The last time I had heard from him was the day I vowed to never speak to him again, but I must admit, I was kinda happy to see him.

He reached in and wrapped his arm around my neck. "Long time no see."

I didn't know what to do or say. Not only was I not expecting to see him, but I was definitely not expecting to have to pay for a basket full of groceries with food stamps in front of him. I thought about leaving the basket behind and walking away, but I was next in line and the cashier was waiting for me to put my things on the belt.

I placed my phone in my pocket and hugged him back. "Hey, how did you know it was me?"

"It's hard to forget a face as beautiful as yours. I saw you when you came in and tried to get your attention, but you looked like you was in a rush," he replied.

I started putting my things on the belt and laughed. If only I would have seen him first, I would have rushed my ass out of there. "Yea, I kinda have a lot going on at the moment."

He stood there for a minute with his hands in his pockets and watched me put my things on the counter. This was awkward as fuck. I had no idea what he wanted, but he looked good as hell though in that olive green Nike fleece jogging suit he had on. On the other hand, my ass was standing there in flip flops, tights, and a cami looking just like my struggle.

When I was done clearing out my basket, I turned around and gave a fake smile. "So, how has basketball been treating you? Have you been winning your games?"

"Yea, it's cool. I can't complain. You know how I do. I let my actions speak for me," he replied.

When I was about to respond, the cashier interrupted.

"Your total is $177.39."

I ignored the cashier and continued to talk to Deron.

"That's great, seems like life has been good to you."

"I wouldn't necessarily say good, but it's been aight," he replied.

"Ma'am," the cashier said. "Your total is $177.39."

I smiled at Deron, then turned to face the cashier. She was standing there with her hand out waiting for my payment. I didn't want to just whip out my food stamp card, but I guess I didn't have a choice. I reached into my pocket and pulled it out. Before I could swipe it, Deron stepped in front of me and pulled out his wallet. He smiled at me, then handed the cashier his card.

"Just put it on here."

I put my card back in my pocket, and started putting my bags in the shopping cart. I was grateful for what he had done, but nonetheless embarrassed. When the transaction was complete, I grabbed my receipt and turned to Deron.

"Thank you, but you know you didn't have to do that."

"I know I didn't, but I wanted to. Besides, you can always save your stamps for a rainy day," he replied.

When he said that, I almost fainted. How the hell did this nigga know I was about to pay with food stamps? I put my head down, then looked back at him. "Deron, don't..."

Deron smiled and licked his lips. "Nah, it ain't even like that love. I saw when you pulled out your card, but it's cool. Look, you mind if I walk you out?" he asked.

I wanted to say no, but I couldn't just shut him down after he had just paid my grocery bill. I started pushing my basket and signaled for him to follow me. When we got to my car, I popped the trunk and started putting my groceries inside. Deron grabbed my hand, and took the bags from me.

"Nariah, it's ok. People go through things. That's nothing to be embarrassed about. That's what it's there for, and I'm not here to judge you. I think I did enough of that."

I crossed my arms and looked away. It was hard for me to look him in the eyes after being reminded of how things ended. Deron grabbed my chin and turned my face toward his.

"Is it cool if we start over? I wasn't the best person in the past, and I know I fucked up in less than a week. But if it's cool with you, I would like another chance to show you that I'm better than that."

I bit my lip and looked him in his eyes. It seemed like he was being genuine, but only time would tell. I guess I could give him another chance. It's not like I had anything to lose anyway. I just didn't want things to turn out the way they did before.

I closed my trunk and put my hand on my hip. "We can start over, but I swear, the first sign of disrespect and it's a wrap. I'm getting too old to play games, and I'm still trying to get my life back on track."

He smiled and kissed my forehead. "I promise you that things will be different this time around. I'm not trying to waste your time or play with your heart love. I wanna show you that I'm really that nigga. Just trust me. Matter of fact, I think you should come to my game tonight. ONLY if you don't have to work. I don't want to put you in a fucked up position like I did last time."

"Oh, you're finally admitting it, huh? But I can come to your game. I am still unemployed at the moment so, I can stay out as late as I want to," I grinned.

Deron rubbed his head and laughed. "Sounds like a plan baby. If your number is still the same, I'll shoot you a text with the information. I tried calling you a couple of weeks ago, but I couldn't get through."

"That's because I have your number blocked," I laughed. "But don't worry, I'll unblock it. I promise."

"Aight love, bet. I'll see you tonight." Deron said as he walked away.

I got in my car and let out a small scream. I couldn't believe that all of this had just happened. I was still a little humiliated about the whole food stamp thing, but I'd get over it. The ending result was enough to make me forget about it. I cranked up my car and put it in reverse.

When I started backing up, I heard a loud bang. I quickly threw my car in park and hopped out. I walked around to the back end, and noticed that I hadn't moved the basket. I guess I was too caught up in the moment. I pushed the basket from behind my car and got back in. Who would've thought that a simple trip to the grocery store would turn into a reunion?

Chapter Six – Deron

Seeing Nariah made a nigga feel good as hell. I had been thinking about her for some time now, so I was happy to be able to reconnect with her. I would've stood out there and talked with her a little longer, but I had something I needed to take care of before my game tonight. Allyson's ass had been blowing me up for the past week and a half, leaving voicemails and texts asking me to please talk to her. The last time I had spoken to her was when I found out about her husband at our meeting. When I said I was done with her I meant it, so I didn't need her showing up to my game trying to cause trouble between Nariah and I.

I picked up my phone to read a text she had sent while I was in Wal-Mart, but before I could open it my phone started ringing. It was her calling again. I let the phone ring a few times before I picked up.

"Hello," I answered annoyed.

"Deron, I need to talk to you. I haven't heard from you in a while. I been worried about you," she said.

I pulled the phone from my ear and looked at it. This bitch had a lot of nerve. I was the last person she should be worried about.

I put the phone back to my ear. "I find it kind of funny that you've been worried about me. You should've been worried about your husband."

"What you mean Deron? Please don't do this. It's not what you think," she replied.

"It's not what I think?" I laughed. "Allyson, you're married. You're someone's wife. When was you gon' tell me about that shit? Before or after you went back to your mama?"

This girl was delusional as fuck. She lied to me about her whole life for almost a year, and was acting like nothing happened.

"Deron, I'm sorry, but you know if I would've told you that I was married you would have never given me the time of day. You know that just as well as I do," she replied.

"Fuck no, I wouldn't have given your ass shit! You're a married woman! What the fuck I look like giving you anything? And the way you went about handling the shit was fucked up! You told me you left your parents' house when you really left your husband! Who the fuck does shit like that?" I screamed into the phone.

Allyson sniffled. "I meant to tell you the truth. I really did, but every time I tried I choked up. I didn't do it to hurt you, Deron. I only kept it a secret because I was really into you. I enjoyed the time that we shared together at the yacht party, and I wanted you to myself. I don't want him Deron. In fact, I never wanted him. I only got married to get out of the hood, but when I met you I started to regret everything. I fell for you, and I fell hard. I thought you felt the same way about me until you brought that bitch back to our crib," she responded.

Allyson continued to cry into the phone. The more she cried, the more pissed I became. She was playing the victim, when in all actuality; it was her own fault that she was hurt. I didn't care about none of the shit she was saying, cuz at the end of the day she did me dirty. She knew I played ball, and was well aware of what I did on the side. So for her to do this shit and risk getting me tied up in a scandal was fucked up. I listened to her cry for a few more seconds.

"At the end of the day shawty, you still lied! Whether it was intentional or not, you still did it. If what you're saying right now is true, then you should've been a woman and told me up front instead of keeping the shit a secret! You could've at least let me decide if I wanted to be down with that type of shit! You fucked up Allyson! And as for that 'bitch' don't you ever fix your mouth to speak on her again. She ain't got shit to do with what the fuck you did! Unlike you, I told you what was up with her the night I took her home! So miss me with that shit!"

"Just answer this, do you love her?" she asked between sobs.

"I don't know her well enough to love her yet, but I know that I don't love you! Whatever we had is dead and I mean that shit! So quit calling and texting my fucking phone, quit leaving me messages on Facebook and Instagram, and quit showing up to my games! We're DONE!" I replied.

Without giving her a chance to respond, I hung up the phone. I wasn't trying to hear any of the webs she was trying to spin. She lied about being married, and about her whole fucking life as far as I was concerned. Nothing that she said was gonna make me change my mind, and I hope that after this conversation she finally understood that. Let her go cry to her husband.

I started my car and turned the music up. Before I could put it in reverse, there was a knock on my passenger window. Being that my tint was so dark, I couldn't really make out who it was. I opened my glove box and pulled out my gun, then rolled down the window. I leaned back in my seat and let out a sigh of frustration.

"Allyson, what the fuck do you want my nigga? And how the fuck you knew where I was?"

She leaned into the car, unlocked the door, and got in. "I followed you here. Deron, I'm sorry ok. Just listen to me for a few minutes, please."

I locked my doors and rolled the window back up, then looked around the parking lot to make sure the coast was clear. I wanted to make sure nobody saw this bitch get in my car. I put my gun back in the glove box and glared at her. "You got five minutes to say whatever the hell you need to say."

She grabbed my arm and turned towards me. "Do you remember all of the fun times we had together before shit got like this?"

"Allyson, I got a game to go get ready for and I don't have time to waste in this parking lot reminiscing on bullshit with you. So if that's what you came to do then I suggest you get the fuck out and go about your business," I replied while pulling my arm away from her.

"Did you invite that bitch to your game just now?" she asked with tears in her eyes.

I looked at her in disgust. "What I do don't concern you my nigga, and quit calling her a bitch. Does your husband know you're here right now? I bet if I call him and ask him, he doesn't. I'm willing to bet money on that."

She sat up straight, then began rubbing on my chest. I pushed her hand back and stopped her. She leaned towards me and tried to rub on my dick, but I grabbed her hand.

"Allyson, it ain't happening. I'm done with this shit, all of it."

She put her finger to her mouth as a signal for me to be quiet, then reached into my joggers, and pulled my dick out. I wanted to stop her, but one of the things she was good at was giving head. Her mouth piece was official, and no lie, I had been missing it. I leaned my seat back a little and adjusted my clothes. This hoe was really about to suck my dick in a Wal-Mart parking lot.

Without saying a word, she moved in and put her mouth on my dick, which caused me to let out a slight moan. "Ahhhh,"

She looked up at me and smiled, then spat on my dick and started licking it up and down. She twirled her tongue around the tip, then went back down and deep throated it. I grabbed her head and pulled it back up. I wasn't trying to nut this soon. When she came back up again, she started kissing and slurping all over it. She turned her head sideways with my dick still in her mouth and looked at me.

"Deron." *slurp* "I'm sorry." *slurp* "Please," *slurp* "forgive," *slurp* "me." Before you knew it, she was bobbing her head up and down at full speed. I leaned back and closed my eyes, and pretended not to hear her. I wasn't worried about nothing that this bitch had to say. I just wanted her to keep sucking.

Allyson then put her mouth on the tip of my dick and started sucking on it like she was trying to vacuum pack my shit. I could feel myself about to nut, so I pushed her head back down and started thrusting my dick down the back of her throat. I looked down at her and watched as she tried to swallow it whole. When I felt my nut about to shoot out, I grabbed her by her ponytail and forcefully pulled her head up. I jacked my dick off on her lips and watched my nut shoot all over her face.

When I was done, I pulled up my joggers and unlocked my doors. She sat up and licked her lips, then looked at me like she was waiting for me to say something. I reached over her and opened the passenger door. She looked at me with a face full of nut.

"Deron, are you serious?"

"Fucking right I'm serious. I didn't ask you to suck my dick." I replied while putting my car in reverse.

"But you didn't stop me either."

I laughed and handed her a napkin from out of the arm rest. "Get the fuck out my car and go clean your face before I call Kenton."

She grabbed the napkin and got out of the car. I locked my doors and backed out of the parking lot. I guess she thought head was gonna make me forgive and forget, but all that did was prove how fucked up she really was. I turned up my music and headed home. I needed to wash my dick and pick up my bag before I went to the Toyota Center. I couldn't half step tonight. My boo was gonna be there, and little did she know she'd be sitting courtside.

*****

When I got home and got myself situated, I texted Nariah the information that she needed to get in the game. I already had everything set up for when she'd get there, so all there was left to do was play my heart out and win her over. I took my shower and packed my bag, then headed to the Toyota Center. When I pulled into the parking lot, my phone started ringing. It was Nariah.

"What's up baby?" I answered.

"Hey, I just wanted to let you know that I'm here. I'm about to cross the street and walk inside now. You got me a courtside seat?" she asked sounding surprised.

"Of course I did. Where else did you think you'd be?"

"I don't know. I just didn't expect to sit courtside," she replied.

I could hear it in her voice that she was blushing, which was a plus for me. If she blushed for courtside seats, I could only imagine what she'd do once she saw the roses and the towel with my number on it that I had waiting for her.

"You should always expect nothing but the best from me. But look, I gotta get in this locker room before my coach starts flipping out and shit. I hope you enjoy the game, and I can't wait to see your pretty face."

Nariah laughed. "Well ok. Thank you again, and good luck babe. I look forward to seeing you on the court."

We ended the call just in time for me to run in and get suited, before coach started giving his pregame speech. Once he was done, it was time to run out onto the court. I was nervous as hell, but ready. This was my first time playing in front of a woman I was interested in, so I was definitely gonna give it my all tonight. When they called my name, I ran out onto the court and looked in the direction of Nariah's seat. She was sitting there with a smile bright enough to light up the Center. I winked at her and got into position.

When I looked to my left, my blood immediately began to boil. Allyson's ass was standing in the middle of an aisle staring directly at me. I put my hands on my knees and dropped my head. I told this bitch not to come here, but she showed up anyway. I knew I shouldn't have let her suck my dick earlier. It was too late for me to do or say anything, so I just said a silent prayer in hopes that she wouldn't mess up what I had planned for Nariah.

Being that I was the Point Guard, I couldn't really watch Nariah as much as I wanted to once the game started. I was able to glance over at her a couple of times during the first quarter, but once the second quarter rolled around I had to keep my eyes on the ball. When it was almost halftime, I noticed that Allyson had moved closer to her. That's when my heart started racing. I didn't know what that bitch had up her sleeve, but whatever it was I knew it couldn't be good.

The buzzer sounded off for halftime, and we were rushed off of the court. I ran to where Nariah was, only to see that Allyson was now sitting right next to her. I pretended that I didn't see her and gave all of my attention to Nariah.

"What up babe?" I asked as I kneeled down beside her.

She turned and faced me smiling, then pulled out the towel that I had coach give her and wiped my face. "Nothing much, just watching you run this ball up. Twenty points between the first and second quarter. I'm impressed."

I glanced over at Allyson then back to Nariah. She was pretending to play on her phone with a blank expression on her face. I knew that must have been awkward for her, but that's what she got for coming here. I stood up and put my hands on my waist.

"You ain't seen nothing yet baby, but aye, check this out."

I walked over to the guy a few seats back who was holding the roses I had for Nariah. I dapped him up and took them from him, then walked back over and handed them to her. When I handed Nariah the roses, her mouth dropped. She jumped up out of her seat and hugged me as tight as she could. When Allyson seen what was unfolding in front of her, her eyes got big.

"Oh my gosh! Thank you Deron," Nariah stated while checking them out.

I gave her a kiss on the cheek before running back out onto the court. "Anything for you love."

When I got back on the court, I peeped over at Allyson who was now sitting there with her arms and legs crossed. She looked disgusted and uncomfortable, which I expected. But that was none of my concern. Maybe after tonight, she would stop showing up here uninvited.

Chapter Seven – Nariah

I was really impressed, but also shocked at how hard Deron was trying to prove himself to me. A couple of months ago, after only two days of knowing each other we couldn't stand each other. Now, it was almost like none of the tension between us had ever happened. It was a wonderful feeling, but I was still going to keep my guards up just in case he decided to flip the switch on me again. When he brought me the roses, I was elated. Even the woman sitting next to me complimented them.

"Nice roses," she said with her eyes still fixed on the court.

Grinning cheerfully I replied, "Thank you. Pink is my favorite color."

She turned her body towards me and extended her hand out, "I'm April, and you are?"

"My name is Nariah," I replied while shaking her hand.

"Nariah, that's a beautiful name for such a beautiful girl. Is this your first game?" she asked.

"Yea, it is," I replied dryly.

She sat up in her seat and rested her arm behind my chair. "Why did you say it like that Nariah? Do you not want to be here?"

I looked at her and nodded. I understood that she was trying to be friendly, but I was also trying to watch the game. The way she was questioning me seemed a little weird. Come to think about it, she actually sounded kind of similar to the Allyson chick that keyed Deron's car.

"Just out of curiosity, is this your first game?" I asked.

She threw her head back and laughed. "No sweetie. This is more like my 10th game. My baby's father used to play for this team. He used to send me roses just like yours, except mine were red. Those were the days."

I gave her a fake smile and continued to watch the game. They were now in the third quarter with only seven minutes left on the clock. Deron was bussing shots left and right, and the crowd was roaring. Ten minutes later, the woman began talking again.

"How long have the two of you been dating?" she asked.

"Deron and I are just friends," I replied.

She laughed and pointed to the roses. "Friends don't get the kind of special treatment that you're getting tonight."

I pulled the roses closer to me and sighed. "We're just friends. If you're interested in him, I can relay a message for you."

She stood up and looked at me. "That won't be necessary, but enjoy the rest of your game.

The woman walked away right before I could respond. I looked up at the scoreboard and noticed that there were only two minutes left in the fourth quarter.

Deron had the ball and was making his way up the court. When he finally made it to the other side, there was less than a minute left. He stood at the three point line and shot. A few seconds later, the buzzer sounded off, and they had won the game.

*****

After the game, I met Deron in front of the Toyota Center. He walked out with his Nike bag on his back and Beats earphones in his ears. I stood there with my roses in my arms and a shy look on my face. When he saw me, he smiled and took his earphones out and placed them in his pocket. He then walked up, wrapped his arm around me, and began walking me to my car.

"Did you enjoy the game," he asked.

I put the roses in my left hand and wrapped my right arm around his back. "Yea, I did actually. It was pretty cool. I hadn't been to a basketball game since high school, so the courtside thing was dope."

"I knew you would have a good time, and I'm glad you did." He replied.

I looked up at him and grinned. "Can I ask you something?"

"Sure. You can ask me anything you'd like," he responded.

"Who was that woman sitting next to me?"

"What woman?" he asked while looking down at me.

"The woman that was sitting to the right of me with the red sweater."

Deron shrugged his shoulders. "I'm not sure, ma. When I was on the court, all I saw was you. I wasn't paying attention to who was sitting next to you."

When we made it to my car, I unlocked the doors and laid my roses on the backseat.

"She complimented the bouquet, then started asking a million questions. She said her baby's father used to play on the same team as you. For a minute, I thought she wanted you. But when I asked her if she wanted me to relay a message to you, she got up and walked away."

Deron stood there pulling at his goatee. "I don't know love. Sounds like she was just an obsessed fan. Did she say who her baby's father was?"

"No, she didn't. I think she said her name was April though. I don't know. I just thought the way she was questioning me was weird. Maybe she was just an obsessed fan." I laughed.

Deron let out a slight chuckle, "Yea maybe so. But um, what you about to get into?"

I leaned against my car and batted my eyes. "Welllllll, I don't have anything planned. Why? Did you have something in mind? By the way, I know this might sound crazy, but how old are you?"

He put his bag down and grabbed my waist. "I'm twenty-six. How old are you?"

"Twenty-four."

Deron licked his lips. "That's cool. Why'd you think you'd sound crazy though?"

"Probably because that's something I should've known already," I laughed.

"True, but last time we started off on the wrong foot. We didn't get a chance to really run it with each other and cover the basics. I mean, we did, but we didn't. You know what I mean," he said.

"Yea, things were kinda crazy the first time around."

Deron pulled me closer to him. "But to answer your question from earlier, I thought it would be nice if we could spend some time together. There's this 24-hour spot a few blocks away that we could go to. I mean, that's if you're up for it. "

I blushed and rubbed his back. "I would love to."

He looked into my eyes and smiled, but it wasn't just a regular smile. He had this sparkle in his eyes that took me away. I knew it would only be a matter of time before I fell for him. Maybe the time that we spent apart did some justice after all. This was definitely not the same guy I had met two months ago. I looked up and he was still smiling. It was almost like he was mesmerized. I playfully slapped his back.

"Deron, are you ok?"

He gripped my waist tighter. "Yea love. I'm straight. I was just admiring your beauty."

I turned my head and blushed again. "Thank you. So are we gonna head to this spot or what?"

"Yea, yea. My bad boo. You wanna follow me there, or leave your car here and hop in the whip with me, or what?"

"I'd love to ride with you. I just wouldn't want your girl to catch us and key your car again." I laughed.

Deron let go of my waist and grinned. "Say man, that girl ain't even in my life no more. Besides, if I had a girl, there's no way you would've been able to even come here tonight."

I could tell that what I said had rubbed him the wrong way. I wasn't trying to upset him or anything like that. I just wanted to make sure that there wouldn't be any problems before I got in the car with him. I grabbed his face while still laughing.

"I'm sorry baby. Will my car be ok just sitting here?"

"Yea, nobody will fuck with your car," he replied while looking down at me.

I grabbed my wallet out of my car and locked the doors. "Then I'll ride with you."

Chapter Eight – Allyson

I sat in my car and watched Deron and his new bitch from a distance. I couldn't believe this nigga was already parading this hoe around on his arm. The taste of his dick was literally still on my tongue. Then he had the nerve to give the bitch roses like he used to give me in front of me. Deron had me all the way fucked up if he thought that I was gonna sit back and just let him play me like that.

I grabbed my binoculars and continued to watch the two of them walk to his car. I already knew where they were going. Deron always took his bitches to the same spot, Katz's. Katz's was a popular 24-hour New York-style deli and bar, and also his favorite place to go after a win. Once they got in the car and drove off, I pulled out of the parking lot and followed right behind them. I was in one of Kenton's SUV's, so I knew he wouldn't suspect anything.

When they made it to the restaurant, I circled around the block before parking. I couldn't wait on side of the road and watch them go in, due to a police department being right across the street from the deli. I waited until I thought they were seated, then drove into the parking lot. I pulled down the visor and checked my hair and makeup in the mirror. My lips looked a little dry, but that was nothing Carmex couldn't fix.

After I applied the Carmex, I took another glance at my reflection in the mirror. I had to make sure that I was slayed before I went inside and fucked some shit up. I grabbed my purse and my phone and exited the SUV. As I crossed the street, I began to think about the way Deron handled me earlier. The thought of me sucking his dick, then getting put out of his car caused adrenaline to fly through my blood; I was on fire.

When I made it inside of the restaurant, I was greeted by the hostess.

"Hi, welcome to Katz's. Table for one?" The young girl asked while smiling.

I looked around the room to see if I could spot Deron and his groupie before answering her. At first I couldn't find them, but after a few seconds of scanning the room I spotted Deron's big ass head. They were sitting at a table on the second floor looking as happy as ever. I looked at the young girl and gave her a fake smile.

"Yes. Sweetheart, is it okay if I get a table on the second floor? I have a few documents that I need to look over for my boss, and one of my colleagues recommended this place. He bragged about how cozy and tucked away the atmosphere was up there, so I figured I'd drop by and check it out for myself."

She picked up a menu and nodded. "No problem. The second floor is indeed very cozy. Just follow me and I'll show you to your seat.

"Thank you."

I followed her through the restaurant and up the stairs. When we got to the top, I looked over to where the two of them were seated. I tapped her on her shoulder.

"Could I get the table over there?" I whispered as I pointed to the table directly behind Deron.

She looked in the direction of the table. "Uh, okay. I guess. Your server will be appear shortly to take your drink order." She handed me the menu and walked away.

I watched her go back down the stairs, then walked over to where the two of them were seated. Deron must have been selling the girl one of his infamous dreams, because she was sitting there smiling and looking as ditzy as can be. I stood in front of the table holding my menu.

"Well, well, well. What a coincidence," I said while looking at the two of them with a devilish grin.

Deron looked up and shook his head. "No pictures please."

He was sitting there looking nervous as hell. Before I could say anything else, his bitch pointed her finger at me and smirked.

"Wow, hi." She turned and looked at Deron who was sitting there with a sinister look on his face. "This is the woman I was telling you about."

He looked at her with a straight face. "Yea, I don't know this chick."

He was trying his hardest to maintain his composure, but as I expected, he couldn't. I extended my arm out to shake his hand. "You must be Deron. Congratulations on your win. You played a great game tonight."

"Thanks," he said.

Instead of shaking my hand, he just left me hanging. My plan was working. His girl crossed her fingers and turned to me.

"Didn't you say your baby's father used to play on the same team?"

"Oh no honey. I said that they were his favorite team," I replied.

"I could've sworn you said he played on the team," she said while raising her eyebrows.

I rolled my eyes then turned my attention back to Deron.

"So Deron, I know you said no pictures, but would it be too much to ask for an autograph?"

He took a sip of his drink, then responded. "Actually, yes it would. I don't have a pen or a piece of paper, and I'm trying to enjoy my time with my girl."

Wow. Did this nigga just go there? Where was his girl a few hours ago when I was devouring his dick? Oh that's right. She was on her way home. That's ok. I had something for his ass. I set the menu down on their table, then reached into my purse and pulled out a pen along with the napkin he had given me earlier.

"Here, you can just write it on this."

Deron looked at the napkin and choked. His girl sat there looking confused. She grabbed the napkin and the pen out of my hand, then handed it to him.

"Give her an autograph Deron," she replied with an attitude.

Deron took the napkin and the pen from her, wrote on it, then handed everything back to me. I opened the napkin and laughed. The nigga had the nerve to make the autograph out to Kenton. As much as I wanted to slap the fucking taste out of his mouth, I just kept it cool and placed the napkin and the pen back inside of my purse. I picked up my menu and smiled.

"Thank you for the autograph Deron. I would love to chat more, but I have somewhere to be in the next couple of hours." I turned and faced the chick. "It was nice meeting you Allyson. I hope you enjoy the rest of your night."

She quickly stood up from the table.

"Excuse me?"

"I said, it was nice meeting you… Allyson. Isn't that your name?" I replied.

I was having a blast picking at the two of them, especially her. She looked at Deron with narrow eyes and crossed her arms. Deron let out a deep sigh of frustration and stood up.

"If you don't mind, I'd appreciate it if you'd excuse yourself."

I placed my hand over my mouth and let out a fake gasp.

"Oh no. Did I say something wrong? I could've sworn she told me her name was Allyson."

Before Deron could answer, the chick grabbed her phone and her wallet and pushed her chair in. "Come drop me to my car. I no longer have an appetite."

She shoulder bumped me, then stormed off.

Deron rolled his eyes and pushed me out of the way.

"Hey, watch yourself." I said sternly.

He ignored me and took off running behind her.

I laughed and dropped the menu on the table, then headed down the stairs. As I was about to walk out of the door, the same young hostess that showed me to my seat stopped me.

"You're leaving already?" she asked.

"Yes, I am. My waiter never showed up, and I got tired of waiting. Maybe I'll try this place out another time," I replied and walked out.

I walked out of the restaurant just in time to catch them leaving. I laughed as Deron scratched off, then shrugged my shoulders. I guess the second floor wasn't cozy enough for them.

Chapter Nine – Deron

I couldn't believe that bitch Allyson had a lot of fucking nerve. Because of her, my first real date with Nariah turned out to be an epic fail. She hadn't said anything to me since we left the restaurant, and I damn sure didn't know what to say to her. I looked over my shoulder, and peeped at her out of the corner of my eye. She was slouched on the door with her hand on her face staring out of the window.

I plugged my phone up to the USB and turned the Bluetooth on. Maybe some old school R&B music would help get her mind off of the bullshit Allyson had pulled. I wasn't trying to lose her like I did the first time, so I was willing to try anything to cheer her up. I searched through my playlists and stopped on Tevin Campbell. I had the perfect song in mind that I knew would make her smile again.

I clicked on the song, *Can We Talk* and turned the volume up. As soon as she heard the beat, she turned and looked at me, then continued to look out of the window. When the first verse started, I took a deep breath and started to sing along.

"Last night I, I saw you standing, and I started, started pretending

That I knew you, and you knew me tooooo. And just like a roni you were

too shy, but you weren't the only cause so was I.

And I, dreamed of you ever since. Now I, built up my confidenceeee.

Girl next, next time you come my way, I'll know just what to sayyyy."

Nariah turned and cracked a smile, then stared back out of the window. I grabbed her hand and continued to sing.

"Can we talkkkk for a minute? Girl I want to know your name.

Can we talkkkk for a minute? Girl I want to know your name."

When the second verse came on, I turned the volume down and pulled over in a Burger King parking lot. I backed into a spot away from the restaurant, then turned the lights off and faced her.

"So you ain't gon' talk to me love?"

She continued to sit there in silence.

"Nariah, I truly apologize for what happened tonight. I don't know if you believe anything I've said to you, but I need you to know that everything I said was true."

She sat up straight and faced me. "It's not that I don't believe you Deron. It's the fact that you had me sitting right next to her at the game the entire time. I asked you if you knew who she was, and you lied to me to my face. Then she showed up at the restaurant like as if she was invited."

Damn. I knew it wouldn't take long for her to figure out that "April" was actually Allyson's ass. I tried my hardest to keep the two of them away from each other, but I guess I fucked up when I let Allyson slob me down. I hated to lie to Nariah, but I had to do whatever was needed to keep her.

"When you asked me about shawty, I honestly had no idea who you were talking about. And when I told you that all I saw was you when I was out there on the court, I meant that. I didn't know that it was her until she popped up at our table. I don't know what it would take to show you that I'm serious about you, but I wish you would tell me."

She sat there for a minute biting her lip, then turned her neck to the side just enough for some of her hair to fall beside her ear.

"Be honest with me. What's the deal with y'all?"

"It ain't shit with us. She was just something to do when there was nothing to do. We was cool, and we kicked it, but that was it." I replied.

"Do you love her?"

Here I was being faced with the same question again. Truth is, I did love Allyson once upon a time, but I was never actually in love with her. There was no easy way to explain that to Nariah, so once again I had to lie.

"No. I never did. I never had any feelings for her, ever." I replied.

She leaned back in her seat and stared at the roof. I didn't know what was going through her head, but I could tell that she was hurt. I reached over and grabbed her face, then slowly began to kiss her. To my surprise, she didn't resist. She pressed her lips into mine and closed her eyes.

I continued to passionately kiss her for as long as she would allow. When she finally pulled away, I sat back and looked at her with a meaningful look on my face.

"What now?" I asked her.

She pulled out her phone and checked the time, then put it back in her pocket. "I don't know, but it's getting pretty late and I have a lot on my mind. I think we should probably head back."

That wasn't the answer I was hoping to hear, but at a time like this, I had to respect her wishes. I licked my lips and gazed into her eyes.

"Aight love."

I sat up and cut the lights back on, then pulled out of the parking lot. I turned the volume back up on the radio, and looked over at Nariah. She was sitting there messing with her nails. When she caught me looking at her, she gave a sly smile that I had never seen before. I smiled back, then focused my attention on the road. Man, I was really feeling this girl.

Nariah was nothing like the other bitches that I had dealt with in the past. She was beautiful, smart, and funny, and she wasn't on no bullshit like the average bitch. What really turned me on about her was the way she carried and respected herself. She kept things classy at all times. Overall, she was a phenomenal woman, and I wanted her in my life.

I pulled in next to Nariah's car and parked.

"Are you sure you're ready to leave?"

She leaned forward and put her face in her hands. I rubbed her back and ran my fingers through her hair. I didn't want her to go, but if she didn't wanna stay, I couldn't force her to. She sat up and stretched her arms out, then looked at me.

"What are you doing tomorrow?" she asked.

I put my fist up to my mouth and yawned, then put my arm behind my head.

"To be honest, a nigga gon' probably sleep all day tomorrow. I might hit the gym later on in the evening, but that's about it. Why, what's up?"

"I'd like to see you tomorrow if that's okay with you," she replied.

"Of course you can see me, love. Shit, you could've come to sleep at my crib if you wanted to. I mean, why wait to see me tomorrow, when you can wake up to me tomorrow?" I laughed.

She blushed and shook her head, then looked at me with her hand on her chin and her nails covering her mouth.

"You're funny."

I smiled and cocked my head to the side. "Nah, I'm serious."

She pulled her hair back behind her ear and grinned. "After what happened tonight, I don't think spending the night at your crib would be a good idea."

"Listen, you will never have to experience what happened tonight again. That's my word. Like I told you, home girl is out of my life for good. It's nothing with me and her, so you ain't got nothing to worry about."

"I hear you," she responded.

I rubbed her back again and looked into her eyes. "Don't just hear me love, trust me."

She looked out of the window at her car.

So what you wanna do?" I asked while still rubbing her back.

She pulled her keys out of her pocket, and picked up her wallet off of the console.

"I guess I'll come, but I'll need some clothes."

"Don't worry about none of that. Just follow me," I replied.

She took her seatbelt off and sat up. "Okay."

I kissed her again before she stepped out of the car. I waited for her to start her car, then pulled off with her right behind me. Despite the shit that went down with Allyson, tonight turned out to be a good one after all.

Chapter Ten – Nariah

Words could not explain the way I felt about what went down between Allyson and me. I had a feeling that something was up at the game, but without knowing how she looked I couldn't really act on it. I wanted to be mad at Deron so bad, because in a way I blamed him for how things played out. But when he kissed me, all of my anger went away.

When we made it to his house, Deron opened both sides of the garage and texted me telling me to pull in. I guess he wanted to make sure that our vehicles were safe just in case Allyson decided to do a pop up. I pulled into the garage and stepped out. A few seconds later, Deron hopped out of his car and closed the garage. He walked around to the side, then unlocked the door that led to the inside of the house.

He opened the door and looked at me. "Ladies first."

I laughed and walked past him, then stood against the wall. He walked in behind me, turned the alarm off, and then grabbed my hand. I followed Deron down the hallway and into an unknown room. When he turned on the lights, my eyes opened wide. I was standing in the middle of a gourmet kitchen.

The first thing I noticed was the metallic appliances, bright white countertops, and dark wood flooring. There was also a huge island bar with the exact same countertop and matching bar stools under large bulb chandeliers. I walked up to the island bar and slowly slid my hand from one side to the other. It was so smooth and shiny.

The second thing that caught my eye was a huge glass wine cabinet. It was standing in a corner to the left of a door. Before I could open the door, Deron stopped me.

"I don't think you wanna go in there," he said as he walked up to me.

"Why? What's in there?"

He cracked a smile then put his hand on his chin. "That's where I smoke love."

"Oh. You smoke cigarettes?" I asked with a disgusted look on my face.

"Not the ones you buy in the store," he laughed. "I roll my own special kind of cigarettes."

I looked at him and grinned. I already knew what that meant, and as long as it wasn't tobacco I was cool. I walked away from the door and leaned against the island bar.

"So are you gonna show me the rest of your house?"

I was too drunk to check out the scenery last time, but I wasn't going to pass up the opportunity to do so this time.

"Of course I will. Would you like anything to drink before we start the tour?" he asked while pointing to the wine cabinet.

"Sure, but I only drink red wine."

Deron grabbed two wine glasses out of the cabinet. "Aight, Miss Red Wine, coming right up."

When he was done pouring our drinks, he handed me my glass and motioned for me to follow him. We walked out of the kitchen and began the tour. He took me around the entire downstairs before we headed upstairs. There was a media room, a massive game room with double glass doors that led to a built in custom basketball court, a large patio with another outdoor kitchen, and a number of other things that are just too much to mention.

Once we got upstairs, we went straight to the master bedroom. I was tired as hell and already a little familiar with one of the guest rooms, so I didn't really mind. When I walked inside of the room, my mouth hit the floor. His room looked like a page straight out of a BedTimes Magazine. Deron really had this place laid out. I walked over to the California king bed, and leaned against it. The wine was starting to get to me. Deron walked over to me and grinned.

"Don't tell me you're ready to go to sleep already."

I handed him the glass and smiled. "I think this wine is starting to kick in."

He took the glass and set it down on the nightstand. "Maybe you need a hot shower to sober you back up."

I leaned forward and put my hands on his shoulders. "Maybe so, but I'll be doing that alone. Can you get me something to put on please?"

Deron licked his lips and smiled, then walked over to one of his dressers. He opened the top drawer and pulled out one of his jerseys. I crossed my arms and gave him a flirtatious look.

"What?" he asked.

"No disrespect, but you really expect me to go to sleep in that?"

He held it up and looked at me. "What this? Nah, this is just for you to walk out of the bathroom in," he laughed. "I'm hoping you'll sleep in your birthday suit."

I grabbed the jersey from him and let out a slight chuckle. "Can you show me to the bathroom?"

He walked over to the other side of the room and opened the bathroom door. He turned the light on then leaned against the door. "Do you need me to show you how to use the shower head?"

I looked at him and walked into the bathroom. "Keep dreaming while I figure it out."

He bit his lip and looked into my eyes before walking away. I closed and locked the door, then stood against it and sighed. Tonight was going to be one to remember.

*****

When I was done taking my shower, I walked out of the bathroom to see Deron sitting up in the bed going through his phone. He looked at me out of the corner of his eyes.

"Enjoyed your shower?"

I walked over to the bed and climbed in. "Yes, it was much needed."

He put his phone down and smiled. "My jersey looks good on you."

I kneeled in the bed and pulled at the jersey from the sides, then looked myself up and down. "Nah, I think I make your jersey look good."

He laughed and pulled me closer to him. I put my hands inside of his and sat on his legs. I was loving the time that I was spending with him. Our chemistry was so intense and definitely undeniable. I wanted Deron, and I could tell that he wanted me too.

He leaned in and grabbed my waist, then kissed me. The softness and warmth of his lips made me want more, so I deepened the kiss and slid my tongue into his mouth. I played with his tongue and teased him. I don't know if it was the wine or what, but I was losing myself inside of his mouth. Deron tasted amazing, and I loved it.

I could tell that he loved it too, because his hands were no longer in mine. They were now roaming my body. He grabbed both of my breasts and licked all around them, then put them in his mouth one at a time. I could feel his dick growing beneath me. I dropped my head back and began rocking my hips as his dick started to throb. He ran his tongue between my breasts and up to my neck, then grabbed it and slid his tongue back inside of my mouth.

A few minutes later, we stopped kissing and Deron flipped me over on the bed. He licked his lips and looked at me with a flirtatious grin. I could tell that he wanted to say something, but I didn't let him. I had waited so long for this, and I be damned if I waited any longer. I signaled him to come closer as I lifted the jersey and parted my legs just enough for him to lay between them, and rubbed on my pussy. I pointed my index finger at him and curled it repeatedly before putting it in my mouth. He stared at me hungrily, then got on his knees.

I rubbed his head as he kissed on my inner thighs. He rolled his tongue up to my stomach, then kissed on my side. I continued to rubs his head, and accidentally let out a slight moan.

"Mmmmm."

He looked up and smiled, but his tongue never missed a beat. Deron started to work his way down, and began to kiss my pussy. I thrusted my hips forward, inviting his lips into my wetness.

"Fuck!" I moaned, as he licked around my clit.

He looked up and grinned with my pussy still in his mouth; my body tingled with desire. Being that I hadn't had sex in so long, I knew it wouldn't be long before I came. I didn't want to tap out this early, so I grabbed his head and pushed myself back further onto the bed. He looked at me and leaned up.

"What's wrong?" he asked grinning.

"Nothing," I lied. I couldn't tell him what was wrong without being embarrassed.

Deron laughed and shook his head, then proceeded to take his shirt off. I bit my bottom lip and narrowed my eyes taking in the sight before me. He was still as fine as ever. I sat up and slipped the jersey over my head, then continued to gaze at the piece of art in front of me. I was mesmerized, but not nearly as much as he was.

Deron looked at my body and pulled me up. I glanced over at his boxers and noticed that his dick was now standing at attention and fully erect. It was thick, circumcised, and had a downward left curve with a huge tip that resembled a mushroom top; just looking at it made me wetter than a faucet. This nigga was truly blessed. He pressed his body into mine and kissed me, as his dick pulsated against my pussy. I grabbed his dick and twirled my tongue around in his mouth, then pulled out of the kiss and gently pushed him off of me.

"Time to trade places,"

I got up on my knees and pushed him back onto the bed.

I crawled between his legs, and watched him lust after my body. Normally, I'd feel a little self-conscious about my weight, but looking at how hard his dick was, I was convinced that he appreciated every curve I had to offer. He grabbed a condom out of the nightstand and handed it to me. I opened it with my teeth and slid it onto his dick. I stroked him up and down to make sure the condom was all the way on, before I went in for the kill.

Once the condom was in place, I licked my lips, closed my eyes, and started to gently suck on the tip of his dick. I twirled my tongue all around it, then without warning, took all of it into my mouth, and began sucking his entire shaft. I looked up at him shyly and batted my eyes as I sucked. His mouth and his eyes were opened wide. I placed my hands on his stomach, and worked my mouth all the way down and deep throated him.

"FUCKKKKKKK!" Deron moaned.

I ran my nails down his stomach and continued to deep throat him. After about ten minutes, I came up for air and spat on the tip, then slurped it all back up. He grabbed my hands and squeezed them, then begged for me to stop.

"Alright love, that's enough," he said while pushing my head up. I deep throated him one more time and twirled my tongue around his balls before coming back up.

As soon as I came up, Deron turned me over and pinned me against the bed. I laid there, as still as ever as he climbed on top of me. He kissed and sucked on my breasts, while rubbing his throbbing dick against my wet pussy. The feeling that I endured as his dick moved across my clit sent chills down my spine. He was teasing the fuck out of me, and I hated how much I loved it.

A few seconds later, Deron turned me over, opened my legs, and grabbed my waist. He then parted my lips with his dick and gently made his grand entrance. I bit my bottom lip softly, as he began to dig deep into my pussy. I wanted to scream, but I couldn't. I was at a loss of words. My body hadn't felt this way in a long time.

I pulled my hair to the side, and looked back at him. He looked at me and smiled, then started digging deeper.

"Oh my goddddddd!!!" I screamed. I threw my head forward and rotated my hips, causing him to slap my ass and to stroke faster. I could tell that he was really into it. Truth is, we both were. The faster he stroked, the more I felt myself about to cum. I gripped the sheets and tried to move forward.

He leaned forward and kissed the back of my neck. "Don't run from me love."

I grabbed the edge of the bed as my body started to tremble. No matter how hard I tried not to cum, it was getting to the point where I could no longer hold it in.

"Ahhhhh! Deronnnn, I'm about to......"

Before I could finish my sentence, I felt my legs start to weaken. I tried to move forward again, but Deron grabbed me. He picked up his speed and slapped my ass, causing my eyes to roll to the back of my head. Before you know it, my body was shaking uncontrollably.

"Deronnn… Deronnnn!" I screamed as I released my juices all over his dick. I threw my ass back on him as hard as I could and fell forward onto the bed.

"Damn girl!" Deron said as he began thrusting his dick deeper into my pussy. He held onto my waist with one arm, then grabbed both of my arms and held them tightly with one hand. I arched my back and bit the sheets. I already knew what time it was.

"Fucccckkkkk!" he yelled as he pushed deep inside of me.

He stroked my pussy a few more times, then emptied his load inside of the condom. I shook my ass on his dick, then laid flat on the bed. As soon as Deron was done, he rolled over onto the bed and laid on his back trying to catch his breath. I turned over on my side and grinned.

"Yea, you liked that, huh?" he asked while trying to catch his breath.

"It was ok," I playfully responded. I was lying though. It was beyond ok. It was fucking magnificent. Never in my life had I experienced anyone like Deron, and the look on my face must have confirmed it.

Deron laughed and climbed out of the bed. "Ok? Girl, I can count all the teeth in your mouth right now. If it was just ok, I don't think you'd be laying here smiling like you just won the lottery or something."

"Like I said, it was ok. All you did was hit it from the back," I replied while crossing my arms. "What was that about?"

He licked his lips and smiled. "Well, I'm an ass man, and as much as I wanted to stare into your beautiful face, I couldn't pass up getting behind all of that." He slapped my ass, grabbed his phone, and walked into the bathroom.

I climbed out of the bed and smirked. I guess I couldn't be mad at him for that. After all, I was blessed with more ass than a little bit.

Chapter Eleven – Deron

I didn't want to sleep with Nariah this soon, but shit, she wanted it as much as I did. What kind of man would I be if I didn't give her what she wanted? I walked into the bathroom, placed my phone on the counter, and slid the condom off. I dropped it in the trash and turned on the shower. I picked up my phone and unlocked it. Damn, a nigga had 22 messages.

I clicked on my messages and seen that they were all from Allyson. I clicked her name and opened the thread.

Allyson: Deron, I know you're with that bitch!!!!

Allyson: Deron, please respond to me. We need to talk!!!!

Allyson: I might be pregnant Deron. Please hit me back!!!!

Allyson: I swear, if you don't text or call me in the next hour I am coming over!!!!

I locked my phone and shook my head. I knew it would only be a matter of time before this bitch started with this pregnancy shit. This wasn't the first time she had tried this bullshit, so I wasn't about to entertain it, especially with Nariah's fine ass over here. I put my phone down and hopped in the shower. I washed myself off, then got out, wrapped a towel around my waist, and brushed my teeth.

When I was done, I grabbed my phone and walked out of the bathroom, then went around to the bed. Nariah was sound asleep. I wanted to wake her, but I knew she must've been worn out after the way I had just put it down. Besides, I needed to get in touch with Allyson's ass before she popped up over here. I pulled the blanket over her and quietly walked out of the room.

I shut the door behind me and went downstairs. When I got downstairs, I fixed myself a drink and went out to the back patio. I slid the door shut, then dialed Allyson's number. To my surprise, she ignored the call. I guess she was with her husband. When I was about to walk back into the house, my phone started ringing.

"What?" I answered irritatingly.

"I guess you got my messages," Allyson replied.

I looked into the patio door to make sure Nariah wasn't around, then responded. "Look bruh, quit playing on my fucking phone. I nut in you twice, and that was months ago. So chill out with all this pregnancy shit! We ain't got shit to talk about. I thought I made that clear earlier. Quit fucking with me Allyson!"

"SO SINCE YOU GOT A NEW BITCH, YOU THINK YOU CAN JUST GET RID OF ME DERON. MY PERIOD AIN'T CAME ON YET! I'M 2 WEEKS LATE MY NIGGA, AND I AIN'T BEEN FUCKING NOBODY BUT YOU!" she replied.

"Bitch you been fucking niggas from the club, AND you're fucking married! So I don't give a fuck about how late you are! Leave me the fuck alone and move on with your fucking life before we have a problem, and if you ever decide to show up to my crib again be prepared to go to jail! I'm not gonna keep playing these fucking games with you my nigga!"

I hung up the phone and put my hands on my head. This bitch was starting to drive me crazy. The only reason I was letting her make it is because her fucking husband was my plug, and because I didn't want to put my career on the line. Other than that, I would've been got my sister to stomp her ass out. I stood outside for a few more minutes before going back in the house. I needed to clear my head and get my mind right.

I walked back inside and locked the door, then went back upstairs. When I walked in the room, Nariah was sitting up in the bed smiling. Fuck! I hope she didn't hear me. I looked at her and grinned.

"I thought you were asleep love?"

She turned to on her side and brushed her hair back behind her ear. "I was, but I woke up when you closed the door. I wasn't in a deep sleep yet. Is everything ok?"

I sighed and walked over to my dresser. "Not really, but I'll be straight."

She rolled her eyes and glanced at me as I put on a pair of basketball shorts.

"Is it Allyson again?"

I laughed and walked over to the bed.

"Nah baby. I'm just worried about what I'll do during off season," I lied.

I climbed into the bed and wrapped my arms around her. I couldn't tell her about Allyson and her bullshit. After what had happened tonight, I knew that it would only make things worse, and I wasn't trying to kill the vibe that we had going.

She moved closer to me and laid her head on my chest.

"What do you mean you're worried about what you'll do?"

"Well, there's a training camp overseas that I've been asked to participate in. Apparently, they want me to help out with various things. I wanna go, but...."

Nariah sat up and looked at me. "But what? You should go."

"I wouldn't mind going. I just wouldn't want to leave you behind," I replied.

"I'll be okay. We haven't made it official yet, so you should be fine."

I looked at her and smirked. "We haven't made it official yet? I thought that's what we just did?"

"What do you mean?" she asked while smiling.

"I mean, I want you to be mine Nariah," I said while looking into her eyes.

She bit her lip and laughed. "Are you serious?"

"Yea I'm serious. Why wouldn't I be? You think I just bring random females in my house?"

"No, but I didn't think you were ready to take it there yet," she replied.

I kissed her neck and rubbed her side. "I'm ready to take it as far as you'd like for it to go."

She giggled a bit, then grabbed my face. "Well, I guess we're official then."

I leaned in and kissed her, then brushed her hair back behind her ear. "Don't guess bae, know. You're mine now, and I want the whole world to know it."

I grabbed my phone and unlocked it, then went to the camera.

"What are you doing?"

"I'm making it official," I said while snapping a picture of us.

She blushed and playfully punched me in the chest. "You could've at least gave me a heads up.

"Don't worry love. You're beautiful regardless," I replied while uploading the picture to all of my social media accounts.

"Let me see the picture," she said while brushing her hair down with her hand.

I turned my phone screen towards her and showed her the picture. I caught her while she was looking at me smiling.

She laughed and laid her head back on my chest. "At least you got my good side. What will the caption say?"

"We don't need a caption baby. What's understood ain't gotta be explained." I said while placing my phone on the nightstand.

"Mhmmm, just make sure that bitch Allyson gets the picture," she replied while messing with her nails.

I tapped her on her lips and laughed, "Don't ever say that name in this house again."

"I'm just saying. You know she's fucking retarded. I'm not trying to deal with her ass anymore because the next time she pulls some shit like she did tonight I can't promise you that I'll just walk away."

I kissed her forehead and held her close to me. "Don't worry baby. You'll never have to worry about her or any other female coming between us."

"Okay, if you say so."

I held Nariah until she fell back to sleep. I knew that there was a possibility that Allyson would become a problem again, especially with this baby stunt she was trying to pull, but I was gonna try my best to keep her away from Nariah. Out of the corner of my eye, I noticed that my phone was lighting up. I reached over and picked it up, then unlocked it. The picture that I posted of Nariah and I was trending on every social media platform, even the Shade Room had shared it.

I scrolled through all of the notifications and seen that there was a message in my DM on Instagram. When I clicked on it, I instantly got mad. It was Allyson's ass playing around again. The bitch sent me a picture of her in one of my old jerseys with the words, "Let the games begin" underneath it. I exited out of Instagram and placed my phone back on the nightstand, then laid next to Nariah. I was glad she had seen the picture, but nervous about what the outcome would be. Knowing Allyson, all hell would soon break loose.

Chapter Twelve – Allyson

Once again, Deron had a lot of nerve. Not even an hour after I told him that I could possibly be pregnant, he went and posted a picture of him and his bitch. That was definitely a slap in the face. He always made it seem like I was crazy, but I was far from it. Yes, I lied about being married however, Deron wasn't as innocent as he pretended to be either.

The main reason why things didn't work out between us in the first place was because he couldn't keep his hands off of me or other bitches. He cheated every chance he got, and when I'd confront him about it he'd flash out, and let the liquor get the best of him. Every time he was proven wrong he would swing on me like I was a nigga, and when I would try to leave, he'd do everything in his power to make me stay.

When I first left my husband, I had no intentions of going back. But once I found out about the situation with Deron and the new girl, I finally had enough. I got tired of fighting and crying and trying to prove to him that I was all he needed. I was tired of feeling used and getting abused. The worst part of it all was that I couldn't talk to anyone about his ways or actions, due to the fear of what would happen to me if he was exposed to the blogs. The only reason I would threaten him was to get him to listen to me and understand, but still he didn't.

I scrolled through the comments under the picture on Instagram and teared up. People were congratulating and complimenting him, and I was just here heart broken and hurt. I have sacrificed so much for this man, and yet he still didn't care. I just didn't understand it. How could someone that you gave so much to just act like you never existed? How could he just deny my child knowing that he was the only man I was giving myself to?

I got up off of the sofa and walked into my bedroom. I threw my phone on the bed and grabbed my purse off of the floor, then went into the bathroom and locked the door. I sat on the toilet and began going through my purse. When I found what I needed, I pulled it out and opened it. I sat there and stared at the First Response box in my hand, then broke down. I didn't want to go through this alone, but I guess I had no choice.

I opened the box, pulled out the pregnancy test, and tore through the wrapper. I looked at the digital test and shook my head.

"Here we go," I said as I slid down my jeans and panties.

I took a deep breath and put the stick under me, then began peeing. When I was done, I placed it on side of the tub, wiped myself, and washed my hands. I flushed the toilet and sat on the floor with a million thoughts running through my mind. What if I was really pregnant this time? Would Deron finally hear me out, and if he wouldn't, how would I explain this to my husband? The timeframe would be completely off, so there's no way I would be able to pass the baby on him.

Five minutes later, I stood up and checked the test. As I read the results, I covered my mouth and slid back down the wall. Just as I had expected, the window on the digital test said *Pregnant*. I ran out of the bathroom and grabbed my phone with tears still running down my face. I sat on the bed and went to the camera, then placed the pregnancy test on my lap and snapped a picture. He wanted proof, so I was going to give it to him. I went to my messages and sent him the picture, then laid down and waited for him to reply.

Twenty minutes went by, and Deron still hadn't responded. I didn't understand why he was ignoring me. Getting pregnant for him was something that I never wanted to happen, so it's not like I had trapped him. He was the one who chose to nut in me the times that he did in. I plugged my phone into the charger and placed it on the nightstand, then laid back down and placed my hands on my stomach. Whether he wanted to claim my baby or not, I was keeping it. But how the fuck would I explain this shit to Kenton?

Chapter Thirteen – Nariah

It had been six weeks since Deron and I made it official, and I was already starting to second guess the relationship. He asked me to move in with him and although I felt that it was a little too soon for us to be living together, he offered to help me get back on my feet and take my financial burdens off of my hands. Now don't get me wrong, he was a good man, and he always made sure I was well taken care of, but I was beginning to see things in him that were starting to rub me the wrong way. It wasn't anything extreme, but it was enough to make me wonder. Like now for instance, Deron had left for practice since 10:00 am. It was now 8:23 pm, and he still wasn't home. Usually, he'd be home by at least 6:15 pm, but tonight his ass was missing in action.

I had been in the kitchen for the last two hours preparing his favorite dish, lasagna. When I realized he wasn't hitting me up like he usually does, I began calling and texting him every 20 minutes or so to see what was up. To my surprise, he didn't answer any of my calls or respond to any of my texts. This was odd, because we always kept in touch with each other throughout the day. I didn't want to jump to any conclusions just yet, but this was not like him and I was now beginning to worry. I put my wine glass down and reached for my phone on the kitchen counter. I dialed his number again, but just like before, the phone rang once, then went to voicemail.

I ended the call and leaned against the counter, then pulled up my Instagram and refreshed my feed. When the page reloaded, the first picture I saw was of him standing outside of the Galleria Mall with his arms around a woman I did not recognize that was posted three hours ago. I took a screenshot of the picture, then went to my messages and sent it to him. This was the third time this week that a picture of him and another female had surfaced. I slammed my phone down on the counter and downed the rest of my wine. I had a mind to jump in my car and drive to the Galleria, but I instead of causing a scene, I just patiently waited for a response.

Another hour went by and Deron still hadn't contacted me. I was now sitting outside on the back patio with a bottle of wine damn near in tears. This nigga had a lot of explaining to do. The next thing I know, the patio door was sliding open. I turned around and Deron was walking out of the house with a smile on his face and a bouquet of roses. I turned back around and rolled my eyes.

"What's up baby?" he said as he walked up to me and tried to kiss me.

I turned my head away from him and stood up. This nigga had nothing but alcohol on his breath.

"Where the fuck have you been?" I asked while standing there with my hand on my hip.

He walked over to me and handed me the roses.

"Why you trippin' love?"

I slapped the roses out of his hand. "First of all, do you know what time it is? I have been calling and texting you all night and you have been ignoring me and sending me to voicemail. And don't say you've been at practice either, because I know you got the picture I sent you. Plus, you fucking smell like Hennessey. What the fuck is going on Deron?"

He looked at me and grinned. "Me and the homies decided to go have a few drinks after practice and slide through the mall for a minute. Stop trippin' bae."

"So you didn't think to stop and let me know that instead of having me wait here all damn night worrying about you? And who the fuck is the bitch you had your arms wrapped around?" I asked irritatingly.

He turned his head to the side and pulled at his goatee. "Nariah, she's just a fan."

I shook my head and smirked.

"It's always a fucking fan Deron! Just like Allyson right? I'm sorry, I mean April," I took a deep breath and dropped my head. "I already know you're cheating on me. The signs are there. You've been keeping your phone on silent, going outside to answer certain calls, staying up late at night to text, and now this. But that's what athletes do, right? Cheat on their women and expect us to just overlook it."

I looked at him, then walked away and went into the house. I slammed the patio door shut and made my way to the stairs. Before I could start climbing them, I felt something hit the back of my head. I turned around to see that Deron had thrown the roses at me, and was now coming towards me with an angry look on his face.

"Wow really?" I asked as I stood there looking at the mess on the floor.

Deron grabbed my arm and got in my face. "Yea really. What the fuck is wrong with you Nariah?"

"What the fuck is wrong with ME? What the fuck is wrong with YOU?" I asked as I loosened my arm from his grip. "Don't fucking touch me!"

I turned around and went up the stairs with Deron right behind me.

"Nariah look at me! I'm not finished talking to you!"

I continued to climb the stairs and ignore him. When I made it to the top, Deron grabbed the back of my neck and pushed me into the wall. I caught my balance before I hit the floor and turned around. He was standing at the top of the staircase with piercing red eyes. I walked up to him and slapped him.

"WHAT THE FUCK IS YOUR PROBLEM DERON?!"

Without saying a word, he grabbed my right arm and pulled me into the bedroom. As soon as we got in the room, I yanked my arm away from him and stood next to the dresser breathing hard. Deron took his shirt and chain off and sat on the bed.

"So you think you're hard, huh?" he asked while looking at me.

I looked at him and instantly teared up. "Deron, look at what you're doing to me! You've been gone all day out with your homies and a fucking groupie! Then when I question you about it, you try to hurt me! I don't understand! Just keep it real and let me know what it is!"

He got up off of the bed and walked over to me. I stood there with tears in my eyes and clenched my fists. This nigga had another thing coming if he thought he was about to use me as a punching bag. He grabbed my arms and pulled me close to him.

"I told you what was up and you didn't believe me. I told you I would never lie to you or do anything to hurt you," he said while looking me in my eyes.

"But you just did Deron! You just manhandled me for no damn reason! And now you wanna act like it's my fault!"

I pulled away from him and ran into the bathroom. I slammed the door and locked it, then sat on side of the tub and buried my face into my hands. This was the first time Deron had ever put his hands on me. I didn't know how to feel or what to do. I had never been in a situation like this before. I sat there and cried until I couldn't cry anymore. If this was what it took to be with him, then I would rather be alone.

I sat in the bathroom for a few more minutes, then washed my face and walked out. When I walked back into the room, Deron was nowhere in sight. I didn't hear him leave, so I knew he was still in the house I just didn't know where. I walked out of the room and made my way down the stairs. My body was killing me, but I needed to save the food and grab the bottle of wine I had earlier off of the patio table.

I walked into the kitchen and saw Deron saving the food. When he saw me, he stopped and stared at me. I walked out of the kitchen and went get the bottle of wine. When I walked back into the house, he was standing near the wine cabinet with his hands in his pockets. I set the bottle of wine on the island bar and just stood there.

"Nariah, I'm sorry for what I did to you. I was wrong for putting my hands on you, and I was wrong for not checking in with you. I promise that I will never ever allow myself to do this to you again," he said as he walked over to me.

I brushed my hair behind my ear and looked up at him with tears in my eyes. "Deron, all I did was ask you a question and instead of answering it, you took things to another level. Do you know how much that hurt? I would've never thought you would do this to me. Is this why you wanted me to move in with you?"

"No love, not at all," he said while placing his hands in mine. "I fucked up, and I'm sorry. I'll never hurt you like that again. Just trust me, and let me make it up to you."

I grabbed the bottle of wine and walked toward the refrigerator, leaving Deron standing there. I opened the refrigerator, placed the wine on the shelf, and began to sob. Deron came up to the refrigerator, grabbed my waist, and closed it. I backed away from him and dropped my head into my chest.

"My father... used to beat... my mother," I cried. "And, I couldn't... I couldn't do anything to stop him."

Deron looked at me with sorrow filled eyes.

"Nariah, I'm sorry. Is she ok now?"

I picked up my head and continued to cry. "My mother... and my father died, Deron. And the way you... the way you threw me into the wall like that, reminded me of just how helpless I was... when it was happening to her."

Deron walked up to me and pulled me into his arms. I had never told him what happened to my mother, not because I didn't want to, but because I just never found the courage to do so. Life was still very hard without her, and talking about what happened to her only made things worse. But tonight, he opened up a doorway to my heart that I had been keeping closed for years, and made me reflect on how things used to be when my parents were alive.

He kissed my forehead and rubbed my back.

"I'm so sorry baby. Please let me make it up to you."

I continued to cry into his arms. There was no easy way to make up for this type of hurt he had bestowed upon me. This was something that I'd have to pray about and sleep on. As I continued to cry, Deron picked me up and carried me into the den, then laid me down onto the black leather chaise. He then got on top of me and looked at me with lust filled eyes, then he began to kiss on my neck. I let out a deep sigh and just laid there as his hard dick pressed against me. If he thought that sex was going to make me forget about the pain in my heart, he was wrong.

He continued to kiss on my neck, then slowly ran his tongue down to my chest and lifted my shirt. When he attempted to remove it, I stopped him. He leaned up and looked at me.

"What's wrong?"

"Deron, do you really think sex is the answer to everything?" I asked while rolling my eyes.

"I just want to make you feel better, Nariah. That's all."

"You can make me feel better by keeping your dick in your pants. We've only been together for six weeks, and you've cheated on me multiple times already. You put your hands on me and threw me around like a rag doll, and now you're trying to make me feel better by fucking me."

I turned my head to the left and placed my hands on top of my head.

"If you really want to make me feel better Deron, just quit doing shit to hurt me."

He pulled my shirt down and got up.

"Bet."

I sat up and watched him walk out of the den. He had lost his mind if he thought that he was about to fuck me after he had just fucked me up. I thought about leaving, but tomorrow we were flying out to Miami for the weekend. Regardless to what had happened tonight, I deserved a trip away from the shit I had been dealing with in Houston. Besides, I couldn't just walk away from him with nothing to fall back on.

Chapter Fourteen – Deron

"Nariah, you ready ma?" I yelled from the bottom of the staircase.

I looked at my Rolex and shook my head. We were supposed to meet my brother at the airport 30 minutes ago. It was now 2:15 pm, and Nariah still hadn't brought her ass down. The nigga had been calling me all morning to make sure we'd meet him there on time, yet here we were still at the house. Ten minutes later, Nariah came running down the stairs with her bags.

"Ok, I'm ready."

I looked her up and down, then grinned. This girl had been upstairs for almost two hours and had the audacity to come down here wearing a pair of orange PINK sweats and a grey V-neck. Then she had the nerve to have on a pair of Ray Bans.

"So you're flying to Miami in sweats and a t-shirt?"

She squinted her eyes and took of her Ray Bans.

"Is that a problem? I'm not trying to impress anyone on a damn plane. You're always the one who's worried about what you have on. *Fans* always want pictures with you anyway, remember?"

She put her shades back down and went outside to the garage. Instead of replying to her, I just grabbed my shit and locked up the house. We hadn't said anything to one another after what went down last night until now, so I wasn't trying to start no bullshit with her ass. By the time I made it to the garage, Nariah had already put her bags in the trunk and was sitting in the passenger seat reading. I threw my bags in the trunk and got in the car.

"I just want to apologize again for what I did last night. I would appreciate it if you wouldn't mention what took place around my brother. I don't need his ass trying to intervene or meddling in my business."

Nariah looked up from her book.

"I don't even want to think about what took place last night let alone discuss it. So you don't have to worry about that. Just make sure you remember what I said."

I started the car and backed out of the garage.

"Yea Nariah,"

She leaned her seat back a little, and began reading again. I wasn't trying to make her think about what had happened. I just wanted to be sure that she didn't slip up and talk about the shit in front of my brother. He was the type of nigga that felt like he knew everything. He was a player ass nigga don't get me wrong, but sometimes he acted like a nigga's daddy and I wasn't with that shit. If he found out that I had put my hands on Nariah, he'd take shit to a level that would only cause more drama that I didn't need on my plate.

When we made it to the airport, I sent my brother a text to let him know that we were about to walk in, then hopped out and grabbed our bags. The plane would be boarding in the next 20 minutes, so we needed to get inside as fast as possible. As we walked inside of the airport, I noticed that Nariah was walking behind me. I already knew what she was doing, so I just kept walking and played it cool. That was her way of letting me know that she was still upset. When we made it to where my brother was, she took off her shades and just stood there.

I walked up to my brother and gave him a bro hug.

"What up bro?"

Shit man. What up baby brother?" he replied while staring at Nariah.

I grabbed her hand and pulled her next to me.

"Nariah, this is Nick. Nick, this is Nariah."

He extended his hand to her and smiled. "What's good Nariah? I heard a lot about you."

She shook his hand and laughed. "I'm sure you have. I've heard a lot about you as well. It's nice to finally meet you."

"So bro, what you got in store for us this weekend? You know I ain't been to Miami in a minute," I said.

Nick rubbed his hands and grinned. "Shit baby bro, that nigga Ball Greezy got a concert at a lil' spot tomorrow night. Today we can hit up the stores and beaches to show your lady around, and Sunday we can just chill until it's time to head back here."

"Cool, cool. How does that sound bae?" I asked while looking at Nariah.

"That's fine, but I ain't hear neither one of y'all say anything about shopping."

"Don't worry about shopping love. You will have plenty of time to do that. My bro ain't got no problems letting you go with that black card," Nick laughed.

Nariah looked at me and smiled. "I know he doesn't. He owes it to me."

I gave her a fake smile, then picked up our bags. A few seconds later, an announcement came on about boarding our plane. I looked at the board on the wall, then looked at Nick.

"Say bro, ain't that our flight they just called out?"

"Shit bro, y'all gotta go check in y'all luggage," Nick replied. "You want me to go handle that or you got it?"

"I got it bro. Just keep an eye on Nariah for me," I said while walking away.

"My pleasure," he replied.

I kissed Nariah and went to check in our bags. I wasn't trying to miss our flight, and I needed a few minutes to myself. My phone had been vibrating nonstop the whole ride here. I put the bags on the counter and pulled out my phone. Just as I thought, I had 52 messages and calls from Allyson. I opened my messages and clicked her name. She was going on and on about this pregnancy shit again.

Allyson: I can't believe you're denying my baby, our baby.

Allyson: Deron, you cannot do this to me. We had an agreement, and I was always good to you. How can you just ignore me like that?

Allyson: Since you want proof, here's your proof. I'm pregnant Deron, and I'm keeping my baby whether you like it or not.

Allyson had sent a picture of the pregnancy test, as well as pictures of confirmation papers from the doctor. I exited out of the message and placed my phone in my pocket. Allyson and her bastard baby were the last things on my mind. If it was my baby, I wasn't claiming it until I got a DNA test to prove it. I wasn't the only nigga she was fucking, so I wasn't about to take a charge that wasn't mine.

I grabbed our boarding passes from the attendant, and walked back over to Nick and Nariah. Nick was sitting there scrolling through his phone, and Nariah was standing there with her earphones in her ears looking irritated. I guess she wasn't feeling the fact that I was bringing my bro along on our couple's trip, but we had business to handle.

I handed Nariah her boarding pass. "Aight, we all set."

Nick stood up and shook his head. "Your girl antisocial, huh bro?" he asked while grinning.

I looked at Nariah and laughed. "Nah bro. She just on some other shit right now, but hopefully this trip gets her mind right."

She looked at me and rolled her eyes. "You don't wanna go there."

Nariah put her earphones back in her ears and walked away. Nick looked at me and laughed.

"She gon' be aight bro. She probably just tired. You know bitches always tired or hungry."

We laughed and walked towards the terminals. If only he knew what was really going on.

*****

We touched down in Miami a little after 5 pm, and immediately checked into our rooms at The Setai Miami Beach. Nick had a couple bitches to catch up with, so that gave Nariah and I a chance to be alone for a few hours. We still hadn't eaten yet, and a nigga was hungry as hell. I looked over at her and smiled. She was standing on the hotel balcony recording a video for Snapchat as I walked up to her and grabbed her waist.

"Feel like going to grab something to eat?"

She let out a deep sigh, then ended the video and moved forward.

"I'm good. I think I'll just order room service and chill here."

"Really Nariah? So you really gonna act like this during the whole trip? Look, I understand you're probably still upset about last night, but damn we're in Miami. I'm not trying to deal with no fucked up attitude all weekend. I brought you here to take your mind off of the bullshit, but if I would've known you was gonna act like this you could've just stayed home."

Nariah scrunched up her face and folded her arms.

"You're fucking right I'm still upset about last night. That's not some shit that I can just get over like that, and trust me I would've stayed home if you wouldn't have been bothering me to come with you."

She walked inside of the room and sat on the bed. This girl was really acting crazy with herself, and was beginning to remind me so much of Allyson. I walked in behind her and stood in front of her.

"Say, if you wanna go back home all you gotta do is say the word. I'm not trying to spend the whole weekend pulling your arm or walking on eggshells. Matter of fact, I can book you a flight right now," I said while pulling out my phone.

Nariah stood up and walked into the bathroom.

"You don't have to do shit. I can book my own fucking flight," she replied before slamming the door.

I sat on the bed and dropped my head into my hands. I was really starting to regret bringing her ass here. I had business to handle, and her attitude was fucking up my vibe. I knew a lot of it had to do with me putting my hands on her, but fuck, I apologized. What more did she want? It was time to let that shit go, and if she couldn't then we would be faced with another problem. I got up off the bed and strolled over to the bathroom. It was just my luck that her crazy ass locked the door.

"Nariah, open that fucking door!" I said while turning the knob.

"Fuck you Deron! I'm going back to Houston!"

I shook my head, then hit the door with my fist.

"Nariah, I swear. If you don't open this damn door, you'll never have to worry about me fucking with you again. I will leave you at this fucking hotel and let you be. I ain't got time for this bullshit Nariah, now open the fucking door!"

She let out a wild, piercing scream, then burst out of the bathroom. Before she could do or say anything, I grabbed her arm and held her in a tight bear hug.

"Chill the fuck out girl. You're doing all this shit for nothing. We're supposed to be having a good time and enjoying ourselves out here, and you're trippin over some shit we're supposed to be trying to get past. We ain't even been out here a whole two hours Nariah. I know what I did was wrong, but damn. If you keep holding on to that shit we ain't never gon' get nowhere. Is that what you want? If not, then please let me know what the fuck I gotta do for you to stop this shit?"

She sighed and turned her head towards me.

"The only way I will stop 'trippin' is if you eat my pussy on the balcony."

I let her go and started laughing.

"Stop fucking playing Nariah. I'm serious."

"I'm serious too. What? You're scared you're gonna get caught eating your girl out or something?"

I leaned against the wall and rubbed my hands together.

"Nah, it ain't that. I just know you ain't serious. A few hours ago I couldn't even kiss you, but now you want me to believe that you're down with some freaky shit like that? Come on ma. You ain't fooling nothing."

Nariah grinned and shook her head, then began taking her clothes off. When she slid out of her thong, she threw it at me then walked outside onto the balcony. She stood against the railing, spread her legs, and started rubbing her pussy.

"Does it look like I'm not serious?"

I dropped my head and laughed. This girl was crazier than I thought. She looked good as fuck though, and she knew just what to do to turn a nigga on. My dick was getting hard as hell watching her please herself, but I knew she wasn't really about that action.

"Girl, bring your ass back in this room and quit playing."

"Deron, I'm not fucking playing. If you ain't got shit to hide and you're as sorry as you claim you are, then come here, get on your knees, and eat this pussy." She said while sliding her finger inside of her hotbox. "If you don't come do it, I'll leave and you'll never have to worry about me again."

She pulled her finger out of her pussy and sucked on it. I thought it was cute how she tried to use my own line on me, but hey, if this was what it took to get her to calm her ass down then her wish was my command. I took off my shirt and walked over to Nariah, then turned her around, bending her over on the rail. I gently kissed the back of her neck and ran my tongue down her spine while squeezing her breasts. When I got to her ass, I slapped and gripped it, then spread her legs and began French kissing her second set of lips.

"Mmmmmmmm," she moaned as her right leg trembled.

Nariah was wet as fuck, and I was gonna swallow every drop of her. I continued to play with her breasts and began running my index finger around her hard ass nipples. She dropped her head to the side and kept moaning as I licked and sucked all on her clit.

"Ahhhh…..shit. Uhhhhhh."

Her sexy ass voice had my dick throbbing, but I wasn't near finished with her. I sucked on her pussy softly, then ran my tongue all the way up the crack of her ass, and all the way back down to her clit. She grabbed the rail and pulled herself up from my mouth.

"Nah, don't run, just chill." I said while pulling her back down.

I ran my tongue up and down again, then started fucking her pussy with my tongue. Nariah was now rocking back and forth and bouncing up and down. Without warning, I let go of her breasts and stuck my thumb in her ass. She screamed and tried to grab my hand.

"Deronnnn, what the fuckkkkk?!"

I continued to finger her ass and fuck her pussy with my tongue, as she lost control of herself. She was getting wetter and wetter and moving faster and faster, so I knew she was about to cum. I stood up and dropped my jeans and boxers, then slid my dick into her pussy.

"Ohhhhhh…fuckkkkkk!" she moaned.

I grabbed her throat and started pushing my dick deep inside of her.

"You gon' nut on daddy dick?"

"Yesssssss! Mmmmm, yessssss!"

She reached around and wrapped her arm around the back of my neck. I let go of her throat and grabbed her waist, then started pounding her pussy even harder.

"Deronnnnnnn, I'm about to cummmmm…I'm about toooo….Ahhhhhhhhh!" she screamed as she slid up and down my dick.

"Nut on daddy dick."

The way she rocked her hips as she let her juices come down had me ready to bust. I grabbed her by her hair and continued to thrust my dick in and out of her creamy pussy. A few seconds later, I felt my dick about to explode.

"Shitttttt…Fuckkkkkk!"

I pulled my dick and shot my nut all over her ass. She leaned against the railing, then turned and faced me.

"I hate you," she said while panting and trying to catch her breath.

I looked at her and laughed, then walked into the room. She could say she hated me all she wanted to, but her pussy didn't though.

Chapter Fifteen – Nariah

I hated how weak I was for this nigga, but what I really hated was how good his dick was. No matter how hard I tried to stay mad, after he put it down it just wasn't possible. The way he stroked me could turn a frown into a smile any day. I walked into the room and went straight to the bathroom. I wasted enough time playing around with Deron and his dick. It was time to go enjoy the beaches and get to shopping. It was gonna take a lot more than dick to make me forget about last night.

I turned on the shower and jumped in. My legs were fucking weak as hell, but man I was feeling lovely. I grabbed the washcloth off of the shelf. Looking around for my body wash, I realized that I had left it in my suitcase.

"Hey babe, can you bring me my body wash, please? The cocoa butter one that's in the side pouch to the left," I called out to Deron.

He walked into the bathroom and pulled the shower curtain back, then handed me my body wash.

"Can I join you?" he asked as he stepped in.

"Uh damn, can I answer you first? How do you know I didn't want to shower alone?"

"Don't make me make you scream again. Deronnnnnn! Deronnnnnn!" He mimicked me, laughing at the same time.

I looked at him and grinned. See, this is the shit I was talking about. It was so hard for me to stay mad at this man.

"Boy bye, I wasn't screaming nothing. Besides, we can save round two for later. I'm ready to sight see and get my Baywatch on."

Deron licked his lips and laughed.

"Baywatch, more like Big Mama? We just gotta get you some braids and a yellow bathing suit, and you'll be good to go."

I slapped his chest with the wash cloth and put my hands on my hips.

"Really bae?"

"I'm just fucking with you bae," he continued to laugh.

"Yea ok, now I don't even wanna go anymore."

Deron grabbed my face and kissed me, sticking his tongue down my throat.

"You know I was just playing baby. I love you, and I will never say or do anything to hurt you again."

I smiled and looked into his eyes. Deron had never told me he loved me before. Not that I was in a rush to hear him say it or anything. I just wanted to make sure he was saying it because he meant it, and not because he felt like it would shut me up.

"Do you really mean it Deron?"

"I mean it baby. I've been wanting to tell you for a minute now. I just didn't know how."

I gazed into his eyes and kissed his lips.

"I love you too baby."

"You better. Now let's finish up in this shower so we can get our weekend started. A nigga smothering and about to melt in here with this hot ass water."

We laughed and began washing each other clean. I couldn't wait to see what he had in store for us.

When we were done in the shower, we dried ourselves off, then got ready to hit the streets. We weren't trying to get too dressed up, but I must say we complimented each other very well. I threw on a Fashion Nova camo jumpsuit with a pair of black Yves Saint Laurent open toe sandals, while Deron was dressed in a washed dark grey and black Yves Saint Laurent t-shirt, camo cargo shorts, and a pair of all black high top leather Yves Saint Laurent sneakers to match.

"You're ready to go babe?" he asked while staring me up and down and licking his lips.

I looked at my reflection in the mirror next to the bed, then smiled.

"Yea baby."

I was looking good as fuck, and ready to slay in these Miami streets. I grabbed my phone and my wallet, threw on my shades, then grabbed my man's hand. We were definitely killing shit.

*****

When we made it down to the hotel lobby, paparazzi was everywhere. I grabbed Deron's arm and buried my face into his shoulder. I didn't feel like dealing with cameras today or the bullshit blogs. Every time we were spotted out, we ended up all over social media. I understood that this was what came with dating a ball player, but I hated being in the limelight. His ass, on the other hand, loved the attention.

"Why you hiding your face?" Deron asked while looking down at me grinning.

"I'm just not feeling it today. Can you walk faster?"

"Nariah, I'm walking as fast as I can. What you want me to do, run?"

"You ain't gotta run, but you can sprint like you're on your way to some new pussy," I sarcastically replied.

"Stop playing girl," he laughed.

When we made it out of the lobby, I quickly jumped in the black on black 2016 AMG G65 Mercedes Benz that Deron had waiting for us. He stood outside for a couple of minutes to take a few pictures, then jumped in and pulled off. I glared at him and rolled my eyes. He shrugged his shoulders and smirked.

"What? I can't avoid them every time."

"You can avoid them as much as you want to, but you don't. And why the hell are we in a rental instead of having a driver?"

"What's wrong with a rental?" he asked while messing with the GPS.

"Ummm, what basketball player drives a rental around in Miami instead of having a driver?"

"One that doesn't want to be seen," Deron replied.

I leaned back in the seat and crossed my legs. "All the more reason to have a driver, stupid."

"Where are we going eat at?"

"It's a surprise. Just know you'll like it."

"I hope so, because I'm starving," I said as I put my earphones in my ears.

I knew he probably felt like I was being hard on him, and I was. I had to though. I refused to just settle and accept less than what I deserve like I used to do in the past. I wasted so much time and energy doing all of the right things for the wrong niggas, and it got me nowhere. Deron needed to get his shit together, so being cold at times was my way of making that clear. If he wanted all of me, he had to give me all of him too.

Fifteen minutes later, we pulled up to the Kimpton EPIC Hotel. I pulled out my earphones and turned to Deron.

"Are you serious?"

Deron let out a deep sigh and threw his right arm up. "What you mean am I serious?"

"So you took me from one hotel to another one to get something to eat? Or am I trippin'? Because this doesn't look like a restaurant."

"The restaurant is on the 16th floor of the hotel. I reserved us a poolside cabana. I know how much you enjoy little things like that, so I was trying to surprise you," he replied. "Plus, I have a few people I'd like for you to meet."

I took off my seatbelt and placed my earphones in my pocket. "What people?"

"Potential future business partners."

"Does everything always have to be about business Deron? I mean really. What do I have to do just to get a few hours of your time to myself? That's all I ever ask for. You know what, don't even worry about it."

"Baby, after this I promise we can go out and do whatever you want to do."

I bit my lip and shook my head. "After this, you can just take me back to the room."

Before he could respond, the valet operator knocked on the window. I quickly took off my seatbelt and stepped out of the vehicle. As I walked inside of the hotel, Deron rushed behind me and roughly wrapped his arm around my waist. I could tell he was getting irritated, but I didn't give a fuck. All I wanted was to spend some alone time with him. He was the one making shit more complicated than it had to be. This was supposed to be a couple's trip, not a family reunion business meeting.

Chapter Sixteen – Deron

Bringing Nariah to Miami was supposed to be a way to smooth things over between us, but it was starting to seem like a mistake. She was complaining and bitching about everything. I know I probably shouldn't have arranged a business meeting this weekend, especially on the first day of us being out here, but I didn't have a choice. I had a shipment that was supposed to come in last week, but it never made it to Houston. So when the plug hit me up and said I needed to get out here asap, I had to do what I had to do.

I still hadn't come clean with Nariah about my side hustle, so that's what made shit difficult. I couldn't just up and fly out to Miami without her being suspicious and thinking a nigga cheating, so I had to bring her with me. I tried to break the news to her a couple of times over drinks, but she didn't understand what I was trying to say. I knew that I couldn't hide it for much longer, but right now I couldn't worry about that. It was time to get down to business.

When we made it to the 16th floor and stepped out of the elevator and Nariah's eyes lit up.

"You like that, huh?" I asked while grabbing her hand and stepping off of the elevator.

As soon as we walked in, all eyes were on us. A host strolled over and guided us to our cabana, then excused herself. Nariah sat down smiling from ear to ear, taking in the scene before her. Being that we were on the rooftop, she had a view of the entire city.

"This is nice babe!" she said as she took off her shades. "The pool is so beautiful and sparkly, and this view is to die for!"

"I knew you would like it, but look babe, the people I told you about earlier will be dropping by soon for a few minutes."

"Just make sure that it's only for a few minutes. Don't make me show out in front of all of these people," she said while rolling her eyes.

"Look, just relax and order you a few drinks. They'll be gone before you know it."

"Oh don't worry. I know they will."

She picked up the menu that was on the cabana and started reading it. As I stood there and watched her, an unutterable feeling of guilt came over me. With all of the arguing and fighting we had been doing, I almost forgot how beautiful my woman was. I was very lucky to have someone like her in my life. I hated hurting her, but I just couldn't get out of my ways and kick my bad habits to the curb.

I mean think about it, I was a young NBA player in Houston, one of the most lit cities in the country with some of the baddest females around. I had been a bachelor for so long that these hoes didn't wanna believe that I was finally with someone. As a matter of fact, to be honest, they didn't give a fuck about my relationship status. They just wanted to fuck, and being that I was always surrounded by pussy, sometimes it was hard to turn it down. It was fucked up, but that's just how shit was.

Nariah put the menu down and raised her eyebrows. I guess she caught me staring at her.

"What?"

"Nothing baby. You're just gorgeous as fuck."

She blushed and continued to read the menu. "Thank you baby."

When I was about to sit down next to her, I heard a familiar voice call my name.

"Money man Deron."

I turned around to see my plug and his wife standing right behind me smiling. Nariah looked up from the menu and stood up.

"Y'all finally made it," I said while dapping him up and shaking his wife's hand.

I grabbed Nariah by her waist and pulled her in front of me.

"I would like for y'all to meet my better half. Nariah, this is Troy and his wife Ariel. Troy and Ariel, this is my girl Nariah."

Nariah waved and smiled. "Nice to meet you both."

"My, my, my, she's such a beautiful girl Deron," Troy said while looking her up and down.

I pulled Nariah closer to me and kissed her on her forehead. "Yes she is. I'd move mountains for this one."

Troy smiled and took off his shades. "Well, who wouldn't?"

"Uhm uhm," Ariel cleared her throat.

Troy looked at her and grinned. "You know I only have eyes for you baby. I tell you what, how about you and Nariah get to know each other while my man Deron and I discuss business?"

Nariah sat back down on the cabana and gave a fake smile. She wasn't really the friendly type, so I could tell she wasn't really open to the idea of socializing with Ariel. I glanced over at her and smiled.

"We'll be right by the bar if you need me baby."

She nodded her head and picked the menu back up. Ariel sat down next to her and pulled out her phone.

"She will be fine. You two run along now."

Nariah smacked her lips and looked at me with a blank expression on her face. I was a little nervous about leaving the two of them alone because Nariah didn't know what our meeting about, but I knew that Ariel wouldn't throw me under the bus like that. I playfully blew her a kiss and walked away with Troy right behind me. When we got to the bar, I ordered us a round of drinks and braced myself for whatever was about to happen.

Without saying anything, Troy pulled out a piece of paper and handed it to me.

"What's this?"

Troy laughed and patted me on the back. "It's what you owe me man."

"Come on man. How do I owe you anything when the package never got to me?"

"Whether it got to you or not, it was addressed and shipped to you. Someone has to be held accountable."

"Yo I get that, but why should I be that someone? I've been doing business with you for years with no problems. Don't let this one mistake come between that," I replied while reading what was on the paper.

Troy wanted a total of $650,000 to be paid to him over the course of the next 4 months for some shit that I never received, and to me that was just plain crazy. He picked up his drink and took a sip.

"You are a great business partner, but I need my money. That's just how things happen sometimes. It's a loss that we both have to take."

"I would be the only one taking a loss, Troy. I'm sorry bro, but I can't agree to this."

"It's not about if you can agree to it or not. Either you will pay me the money or you will have to suffer the consequences, and I know you don't want that."

I laughed and turned to Troy. "Wait a minute, are you threatening me, fam?"

"I'm not threatening you at all. I just don't think you are the type to put your woman in harm's way. That is all I'm saying."

I looked over at Nariah and Ariel who were now laughing and drinking. I wasn't the type to put her in harm's way, but I wasn't no sucker ass nigga either. Troy was on some other shit if he thought I was gonna let him bully me out of my money. For all I knew, he could've kept the shit and made the whole story about it being missing up. I looked back at Troy and laughed again.

"My woman ain't got nothing to do with this, and I don't either. Your shit ain't came to me bro, so I'm not about to pay you nothing. Now we can put this shit behind us and move forward on another deal, or we can just walk away from everything like two men with respect."

Troy stood up and smiled. "You may not pay anything now, but eventually you will. This meeting is over, and so is the business between you and I. I'll be keeping in touch."

He walked away and moved in the direction of where Ariel and Nariah were sitting. I go up from the bar and followed him. When we made it back to Ariel and Nariah, Troy grabbed Ariel's drink out of her hand and threw it to the ground.

"Let's go."

With a confused look on her face, Ariel jumped up. "What was that about Troy?

"We will no longer be affiliating with these people."

Nariah stood up with a disgusted look on her face. "What do you mean these people? You know nothing about me."

"That is true, but we'll meet again," Troy said with an evil grin on his face.

He pulled Ariel by her arm and they walked away. Nariah looked at me and put her hand on her hip.

"What the hell is that supposed to mean?"

Nothing," I said while looking her in her eyes.

She crossed her arms and pointed her finger in my face. "So you're not gonna find out? The way he said that shit was weird. It was almost as if he was hitting on me."

I wrapped my arms around her and rubbed on her ass. "Nobody was hitting on you baby. Calm down, and let's get back to enjoying us."

She cracked a smile, then sat back down. I knew exactly what Troy meant, but there was no way I was gonna let anything happen to Nariah. What was going on between he and I was my issue, and I was going to make sure it remained that way. I sat next to my girl and pulled out my phone. I hadn't heard from Nick since we went our separate ways, and after the meeting between Troy and I, I needed to put him on game so we could figure out our next move.

Chapter Seventeen – Nariah

After Deron and I were done at the restaurant, we went sight-seeing for a couple of hours. We took a few pictures, balled out at a few stores, and then made our way back to the room by 10 pm. If it was up to him, we would've still been out and about, but after the situation with Troy I just wanted to relax and collect my thoughts. I knew Deron was hiding something, but tonight was going to be the night he came clean.

I walked out of the bathroom after taking my shower and laid next to him. As always, he was sitting on the bed playing with his phone.

"So, I'm gonna ask you a question and I expect you to be 100% honest with me."

Instead of answering me, he just kept playing on his phone. I slapped his phone out of his hand and stared at him.

"Do I have your attention now?"

"You had my attention when you came out of the bathroom, Nariah. What the fuck you did that shit for?"

"Because you act like you didn't hear what I said. So I'll say it again. I have a question to ask you, and I want the truth."

Deron leaned back against the headboard and looked at me. "What's your question Nariah?"

"Don't say it like that."

"Don't say it like what?" He asked with an attitude.

"Like if you're irritated. Cuz truth be told, I'm the one who should be irritated."

"Nariah, ask what you gotta ask man."

I sat up and crossed my legs and closed my plush robe. "What was the meeting between you and Troy really about earlier?"

He pulled at his goatee, which he always did before he got ready to lie, and sighed. "It was about business."

"What kind of business Deron? I'm tired of hearing you throw the word business around without putting any meaning behind it. So tell me what kind of 'business' were y'all discussing?"

"Just some basketball shit Nariah. It wasn't nothing serious."

"I told you not to lie to me, and you're doing it anyway. You think I don't know what you do? You really think I'm that stupid to where I can't put two and two together? I'm trying to give you a chance to tell me the fucking truth, and you're sitting here lying to me once again."

"I ain't lying to you about shit. You asked me a question and I answered it. What else you want me to say?"

"I want you to tell me what the fuck you do besides play basketball, and I want you to tell me why the fuck you've been lying to me about the shit."

Deron got out of the bed and started putting his shoes on. I knew what he was about to try to do. He was going to try and run away like he always did, but he wasn't gonna do it tonight. I was tired of being lied to. I jumped out of the bed and ran around to his side. I picked up his phone and his other shoe, then ran and blocked the door.

"Nariah, give me my phone and my fucking shoe. I'm not in the mood to play these games with you. You asked me a question, and I answered you. So just give me my shit so I can go cool off somewhere."

"So you told me the truth?"

Deron turned his head to the side and took a deep breath. "Nariah…"

"No, fuck that, don't say my name. If all y'all was discussing was basketball shit, then why the fuck did Ariel tell me you lost some fucking drugs that belonged to Troy?"

"WHAT?!" he yelled.

"Deron, don't act surprised. Come on now, I been knew what you were doing. I'm not stupid, and you're not as slick as you think you are. So why the fuck are you still lying to me?"

"Nariah give me my shit so I can leave bruh. I ain't even about to entertain this stupid shit."

"I'm not giving you shit until you tell me what the fuck is really up. I'm tired of all of these fucking lies and secrets. It's to the point where I don't know who the fuck

I'm dating anymore. Every time I turn around, I'm finding out some new shit. It's either a new bitch or a new secret, and you're always lying about. I'm so sick of your shit."

I threw his shoe at his face and dropped his phone on the floor.

"Now pick your shit up," I said as I walked away.

"Really Nariah?" Deron asked while wiping his mouth.

"YES REALLY! I'M TIRED OF THIS SHIT! ALL I EVER ASK YOU TO DO IS BE HONEST! YOU BROUGHT ME ALL THE WAY OUT HERE THINKING THAT WE WERE GONNA BE ABLE TO SPEND TIME TOGETHER AND ACTUALLY HAVE FUN, BUT REALLY YOU CAME OUT HERE FOR A MEETING WITH THE FUCKING PLUG THAT YOU OWE MONEY TO CUZ YOU LOST HIS WORK! NOW THIS NIGGA THREATENING ME BECAUSE OF YOU! AND YOU WANNA ASK ME REALLY!! FUCK YOU DERON! I'M LEAVING MIAMI FIRST THING IN THE MORNING, AND I'M LEAVING YOU! ALLYSON AND ALL OF THESE OTHER BITCHES CAN HAVE YOU! I HAVE ENOUGH!"

I walked over to the closet and grabbed my bags.

"So you're really leaving behind some shit another bitch told you?" Deron asked while walking up to me. "You don't even know this hoe!"

I threw my bags on the bed and went around him, then into the bathroom. When I turned around to walk out he was standing right behind me.

"Deron, get the fuck out of my way. I don't have shit to say to you, and I don't wanna hear nothing you gotta say. When you were supposed to be talking, you were keeping secrets. All you do is lie."

He grabbed my wrists and threw me against the toilet, then stood over me as I hit the floor.

"I TOLD YOU WHAT THE FUCK IS UP! YOU'RE STEADY RUNNING YOUR FUCKING MOUTH ABOUT WHAT ANOTHER BITCH SAID INSTEAD OF LISTENING TO YOUR MAN!"

"FUCK MY MAN!" I said while trying to get up. "ALL HE EVER DOES IS LIE TO ME LIKE I AIN'T SHIT, SO FUCK HIM!"

Deron pushed me back down and started punching me in my chest. I threw my hands up in front of my face to block him from hitting me in my face. I couldn't believe that he was doing this to me again all because he got caught in his lie. I pulled myself up on the toilet and kicked him in his face. Deron dragged me out of the bathroom and threw me on the bed.

"IS THIS WHAT THE FUCK YOU WANT? I TOLD YOU TO STOP FUCKING PLAYING WITH ME NARIAH!"

I looked at Deron with tears in my eyes. "You are fucking sad, and I'm done with you. I don't care what or who you do anymore. Once we get back to Houston, I'm leaving you."

Before he could respond, the hotel phone started ringing. I slid across the bed and tried to get to the phone. Deron threw his arm back and slapped me, then answered.

"Hello."

I guess it was someone from the front desk calling, because he began trying to assure them that everything was ok.

"Yea, I'm fine. My lady and I had a small disagreement, but everything is cool. I appreciate you for calling, but we aren't in need of any assistance."

I sat on the bed with my hand on my face and listened to him. Deron was a natural born liar with more issues than the average person. I don't know how I didn't see that from the jump. I got out of the bed and ran to the bathroom. I looked at myself in the mirror and immediately started crying. The right side of my face was red and burning, there were bruises all over my chest, and my mental state of mind was fucked up.

I grabbed a washcloth and wet it, then held it against my face. As soon as Deron hung up the phone, he started beating on the door.

"Deron just leave, please."

"You ain't gotta open the door. Just know that when I come back you better be in that bed sleeping. The conversation between us about whatever the fuck Ariel told you is over. Believe what you want, just keep that shit to yourself. And next time you decide to throw some shit at me, you might wanna think twice. I'm out man. I'll be back later."

He walked away from the door and left the room. I sat in the bathroom for five more minutes then walked out. I didn't know where he was going, and I didn't care. I just knew that when we got back to Houston, I was gonna pack my shit and get as far away from him as I could. I climbed in the bed and pulled the comforter over me. As soon as I got comfortable, there was a knock at the door.

I walked over to the door and looked in the peephole. On the other side of the door, Nick was standing there smiling. I opened the door, and stood there with the towel on my face.

"Deron isn't here."

Nick walked in and stood against the wall. "I know he isn't. I came to talk to you."

I closed the door and locked it, then sat on the bed. He walked over and sat next to me, then grabbed my face.

"What happened to you, bae?"

"What do you think happened?"

Nick grabbed the towel and began dabbing the side of my face. "Why didn't you call or text me?"

"How was I gonna call or text you with him punching on me? I'm really getting tired of him, and I honestly don't know how much longer I can put up with this."

"Don't worry, after this weekend you won't have to deal with it for too much longer. Did you find out anything about the meeting with him and Troy?"

I turned to Nick and broke down.

"Nick, I can't discuss this right now. Look at me! This man whipped my ass like a slave, and you're questioning me about what I found out."

He put the towel down and pulled me into his arms. "Nariah, the only way this will stop is if you work with me. I'm not trying to put pressure on you at a time like this, but I need to know what's up."

"All I know is that he owes Troy money for a deal gone bad. I don't know how much, and I don't know anything about the deal."

"Did you hear Troy say that or did Deron tell you that?"

"Deron didn't tell me anything, and I never spoke to Troy. Troy's wife told this to me. When I asked Deron about it when we got back here, he flashed out so I'm assuming that it's true."

Nick shook his head, then stood up and handed me the towel. "Listen Nariah, I'm sorry for what he did to you, and I promise that you won't have to put up with this for too much longer. I wish I could stay and comfort you, but you know it won't be long before he comes back."

I looked up at him with tears running down my face. "So that's it? You're just gonna leave?"

"Don't do that to me love," he said as he kissed me on my cheek. "I can't stay, and you know that."

I stood up and walked over to the door, then opened it. "It's okay. I understand."

"I'll see you tomorrow night when we go to the club. Just try to get some rest and find a way to get that shit off of your mind," Nick replied while walking out of the room.

I closed the door and got back in the bed. I placed the towel on my pillow, then lied down and closed my eyes. I knew it was wrong of me to mess with Nick behind Deron's back, but when I found out about him cheating on me I no longer cared. I had feelings too, and Nick understood that. I just wish that there was a way for us to be together without having to worry about Deron.

Chapter Eighteen – Deron

"Can you hurry up?" I asked Nariah as I stood waiting by the door.

We were supposed to be on our way to the club, but as always, Nariah still wasn't ready. She walked out of the bathroom wearing a Jonathan Simkha tier-sleeved black lace bodysuit and a pair of black Sergio Rossi Virginia suede over-the-knee boots. She looked good as fuck in that body suit, but I wasn't really comfortable with her wearing that.

"Where is the rest of your clothes?"

She looked at me and rolled her eyes. "That's the only thing I had that would cover the bruises you left on my chest."

"About that, Nariah I'm…"

"You don't need to apologize. Let's just go," she said while walking out of the room.

I knew she was still upset, and she had every right to be. I had fucked up again, and this time was worse than before. I walked out of the room and caught up to her.

"Can we at least not let what happened last night cause any problems tonight?"

She stopped walking and looked at me. "I'm over last night. I just want to enjoy my last night in Miami without any interruptions."

"I feel you. I just want you to know that you're an amazing woman, and I'm sorry for…"

"Deron, just… don't do that."

"Don't do what?"

"Don't tell me you're sorry. If you were truly sorry, you would stop doing it."

Nariah walked away. I shook my head and put my hands in my pockets. Shawty had me feeling bad as shit. When we got in the elevator, I tried to hold her hand. She pulled her hand back from me and stared straight ahead the entire time. Yea, I had really fucked up.

On the way to the club, I tried to talk to her again. She ignored everything I said, and just sat there looking out of the window like she did the night that Allyson showed up at the restaurant. When we pulled up to the club, I parked and turned off the ignition.

"Nariah, we can't keep going like this. I mean, you're not saying shit to me ma. If that's how it's gonna be once we get inside then we might as well just book a flight and head back to Houston tonight. I don't need nobody speculating and starting rumors cuz we ain't talking to one another."

"I'm not mad at you and I won't create a scene, so there won't be nothing for people to say. I just honestly don't have anything to say to you."

"But how does that look? We in the club together not speaking to each other."

"It doesn't matter how it looks. People will talk regardless, so I don't understand why you're even worrying about that. Like I said, all I want to do is enjoy my last night in Miami without interruptions. That's it. I don't want to argue or fight. I just want peace."

"Whatever you say shawty," I said while getting out of the car.

I went around and opened the door for her. She stepped out and walked around me. I closed the door, then pulled out my phone to let Nick know we were here. When we got to the door, the bouncer let us in and Nick was waiting for us. We strolled through the crowd and went straight to V.I.P.

"What's good bro?" Nick asked while dapping me up.

"Shit bro, just trying to clear my mind."

"I feel you bro. I'm trying to do the same thing."

Nick handed me a bottle of Hennessey XO, then turned to Nariah.

"You aight, sis?"

Nariah smiled. "Yea, I'm cool. I'm just a little sleepy, but I'll be okay once I start vibing to the music."

"That's what's up. You look good tonight baby girl."

"Thank you."

I looked at the two of them, then poured me a glass. Yesterday they didn't have two words to say to each other at the airport, but now they were talking like if they were the best of friends. I took my drink to the head, then poured me up another one.

Nick laughed and tried to take the bottle from me. "Slow down bro, the night is still young."

"I'm good nigga. I know my limit," I replied while downing my second drink.

Nariah sat down and pulled out her phone, then began taking pictures of herself. She was really acting like nothing was going on between us, which was cool but awkward at the same time. She was acting like I wasn't there. I looked down at her and grinned.

"Really babe?"

"Yes really. I need new pictures for my social media sites."

I poured me another drink and sat next to her.

"You mind if I take a couple with you?"

Nariah held her phone to her chest and looked at me.

"Uhhh, yes I do mind."

I stood up and turned to Nick. "I'm about to go walk around for a minute bro and just peep out the scene. Take care of my girl for me."

Nick nodded his head and sat next to Nariah. I walked away and made my way through the crowd. Shawty was bugging, and I didn't have time for it. Since she wanted to act like she didn't need a nigga, I decided to call someone who did. I walked outside and went to the car. I got in and locked the door, then leaned back in the seat and pulled out my phone. I found Allyson's name in my call log and hit send.

"Hello," she answered.

"Can you talk?"

"Yea, I can talk. Is everything ok?"

"Yea, everything is everything. I got your messages. I didn't want you to think that I was ignoring you cuz I didn't have a chance to hit you up. I had a lot of shit going on. Being that it's off season, I've been trying to catch up on a few things."

"It's cool," she replied dryly.

"So, how's the baby?"

She took a deep breath before responding. "Deron, why are you calling me? Don't you have your woman to worry about?"

"My child is more important than any bitch walking this earth."

"Your child?" she laughed. "Deron, you have been denying my child since I told you I was pregnant."

"I know I have and I'm sorry. What I gotta do to make it up to you?"

"You can come to the hospital and take a DNA test once the baby is born."

I sat up and put my hand on my head. "What you mean I can take a DNA test. So wait up. Now that I'm claiming my baby, you wanna slap a nigga with a DNA test?"

"Yes, because I don't want you to change your mind later on and say that it isn't yours once you get mad at me again or once you and your girl are back on good terms."

"What you mean once me and my girl back on good terms? We're good now."

"No y'all aren't Deron. If y'all were on good terms, we wouldn't be on the phone right now. You do this every time she pisses you off, and I'm not falling for it anymore. So you can either man up and take the DNA test, or I'll reach out to Nariah myself and let her know everything."

"Allyson don't do this. I'm trying to be a part of the baby's life. Why you gotta make shit so difficult?"

"You made it difficult when you turned your back on me. Bye Deron."

I hit the steering wheel and leaned back into the seat. I wasn't expecting the call to turn out the way it did, and I damn sure as hell wasn't expecting Allyson to come at me about a fucking DNA test.

Chapter Nineteen – Nariah

I didn't even notice that Deron had walked out of the club until I looked around and didn't see him. I was glad that he wasn't around though, because that gave me a chance to talk to Nick's sexy ass. Don't get me wrong, my man was fine as hell, but his brother took the cake. He was light skinned with light brown eyes, long ass dreads, and a slim framed body full of tats. He also had a top grill laced with diamonds that shined every time he opened his mouth. One thing that drew me to him was the fact that he reminded me of one of my celebrity crushes, DJ Esco.

Nick had a swag that was always on a hundred, but tonight his shit was on a thousand. He had on a Bee star cotton Duke Gucci shirt, a pair of black Gucci wool shorts, with the leather slip on Gucci bee sneakers to match. He was also wearing my favorite scent for men, Acqua Di Gio by Giorgio Armani. Call me crazy, but I had already undressed him with my eyes at least ten times since I got here, and I could tell by the way he was looking at me that he was now doing the same. I looked at him and winked.

"How you doing tonight?" he asked smiling.

I took a sip of my drink and smiled back. "I guess I'm okay. I could be better though."

"Oh is that right?"

"Yea," I blushed.

Nick sat next to me and sat his drink on the table. "Are you feeling better?"

"Not really, but I guess I gotta make the best of it."

"You will be alright love. You just gotta think positive and focus on the bigger picture."

I smirked and looked him in his eyes. "What bigger picture?"

"You know what I'm talking about. What's understood ain't gotta be explained."

"Well I don't understand, so I need you to explain."

"All I will say is, a street nigga and a NBA nigga are two totally different things. Don't bargain for more than you can handle."

I laughed and took a sip of my drink. "So you're a street nigga?"

"I wouldn't say all that. I'm just a different breed."

"Oh good, cuz I was about to say."

"You was about to say what?"

"I lost my parents to the streets, so I try to stay away from people who are always in them."

"I'm sorry to hear that love, but that's something you'll never have to worry about with me. I have people put in place to make sure I never have to be out there."

I smiled and looked out onto the dance floor.

"Could you excuse me for a minute?" I asked while getting up.

I slowly walked out of V.I.P. and made my way down the stairs. As I pushed through the crowd, my blood began to boil. Deron's ass was in the middle of the floor dancing on some bitch. When I made it to where they were, I stood there for a minute and watched them. When the girl saw me standing there, she tapped Deron on his shoulder and pointed to me. He looked up and saw me and quickly tried to get to me.

I turned around and stormed out of the club.

"NARIAH!" he yelled.

When I made it outside, I walked to the end of the driveway and tried to flag down a cab. Deron ran up behind me and grabbed my waist. I could smell the alcohol on his breath.

"Deron, let me go. Please, just let my arm go. I'm taking a cab back to the room, and I'm calling it a night."

"Nariah, what you saw was nothing. I wasn't even trying to dance on the bitch."

"I don't care Deron. Honestly, I don't. I just really want to get back to the room."

"I can take you back to the room baby," he said while pulling on my arm.

"Deron stop. You're drunk and you're drawing attention to yourself," I said while looking around.

There was a small crowd of people standing in the parking lot with their phones out watching and recording us. I guess when everyone saw Deron and I run out of the club they decided to tag alone to get their 15 minutes of fame.

"I'm not drunk baby. Just let me take you back to the room."

"Deron, I'm not getting in the car with you like this. You need to call Nick."

"What I need to call him for? I'm your man. You fucking Nick or something?"

"Are you serious dude?" I asked while walking away from him.

I ran back inside of the club and found Nick.

"I need you to come outside now. Your brother is drunk as hell and trying to drive."

Nick threw his glass on the table and followed me outside. By the time we made it back outside, Deron was standing in the middle of the parking lot with his arm wrapped around a different female. I shook my head and walked to the car, while Nick went and got him. When they made it to the car, Nick unlocked the doors and handed me the keys.

"I'm not driving this car," I said while handing them back to him.

He put Deron in the passenger seat, then handed the keys back to me.

"Nariah, I'll follow y'all to the room."

I grabbed the keys from him and got in the car. I looked over at Deron, who was leaning back in the seat with his eyes closed and his arm behind his head. I wanted to choke the fuck out of him, but I just started the car and drove off. I looked in the review mirror to make sure Nick was behind me. There was no way I was about to deal with this drunk ass nigga alone.

When we made it back to the hotel, Nick helped me get Deron out of the car and into the room. As soon as we got in the room, I threw Deron's arm off of me and began pacing back and forth. Nick dropped him on the bed, placed his phone on the desk, and looked at me.

"Nariah, calm down."

"Calm down! This nigga just embarrassed both me and him in front of everyone. People were taking pictures and recording his every fucking move. I bet social media is having a field day with his ass right now."

"Yea, but don't worry about that. That shit will blow over in a couple of days. Athletes get fucked up all the time. You know how that goes."

"That's not the point Nick. The point is if I knew he was coming out here to act a fucking fool, I would've stayed my ass in Houston."

"I feel what ya saying, but we leaving tomorrow so just chill. I gotta get back to the club to pick up a friend of mine that rode there with me. If this nigga wake up before tomorrow, tell him to call me."

"Will do," I said while cracking a fake smile.

Nick walked out of the room and closed the door. I locked it and gathered my things to get ready for bed, then walked into the bathroom. I took off my clothes and washed my body. When I was done taking my shower, I dried myself off, wrapped my hair, and slipped into my Adore Me Ellis robe. I walked out of the bathroom and climbed in the bed next to Deron, who was still sound asleep.

Out of the corner of my eye, I noticed that Deron's phone kept lighting up. I quietly climbed out of the bed and walked over to the desk. I picked up his phone, only to see that it was locked. I tiptoed to the bed and put the phone under his hand, then gently pressed his index finger onto the screen. Once the phone was unlocked, I slid it out from under his hand and walked around to my side of the bed.

I sat on the floor and began going through his messages. Skimming through them confirmed everything that I already knew. Deron was talking to a plethora of bitches. He was sending them pictures of his dick, setting up dates with them, and even offering some of them money for sex. But the thread that caught my attention Allyson's.

I clicked on it and began scrolling. As I read through their messages, my eyes began to water and my chest began to tighten up. Allyson was pouring out her heart to him and he was doing the same. He even went as far as calling me a rebound. I scrolled a little more, and almost screamed. Allyson had sent him a picture of a pregnancy test and confirmation papers the day we left to come out here, and according to her the baby was his.

"She's pregnant for him," I quietly said to myself.

I felt my heart shatter. I exited out of the messages, then closed all of the open apps and powered it down so that he wouldn't notice that I went through it. I placed it back on the desk, grabbed my shoes and the room key, and walked out of the room. As soon as I closed the door, the tears began to fall. This whole time, Deron had me believing that he and Allyson were done, when in all actuality they were still fucking around and even expecting a baby.

I could not believe him. When I got in the elevator, I stood against the doors and cried my eyes out. I was hurt, and I didn't know what to do. I just knew that I needed to talk to someone I could trust. When I got off of the elevator, I power walked through the lobby and went outside to call Nick. I knew he wouldn't answer for me at this time of night, so I decided to call private.

"WHO THE FUCK IS THIS?!" he screamed into the phone.

"It's me," I cried.

"Nariah?"

"Yes, I really need to talk to you. I'm outside of hotel and…"

"Wait what? What are you doing outside of the hotel? Where's Deron?"

"He's in the room. Just, please come and meet me in the courtyard."

"What you mean he's in the room? Are you locked out or something? Cuz I can call him and let him know."

"No, no, no. Please don't call him, Nick. I just really need to talk to you. Please!" I begged.

"Aight, I'm coming down now. Let me put some clothes on, and I'll be down there in a minute."

I hung up the phone and buried my face into my hands and continued to cry. The person that I had grown to trust and love was not only cheating on me and abusing me, he also had a fucking baby on the way. A baby with a bitch he claimed meant nothing to him. A baby with a bitch that he told me not to worry about. A baby with a bitch that tried to destroy us before we were even an item.

*****

When Nick finally came outside, I jumped up and ran into his arms. I could barely talk to him without crying. He held me close to him as I cried in his chest.

"Nariah, what's wrong? Did somebody do something to you?"

"It's Deron."

"What? Did he beat you again?"

"No," I cried.

"Well, what happened? I need you to stop crying and tell me what's up ma. You standing out here in nothing but a robe on and shit. What the fuck going on?"

I pulled away from him and wiped my face with my hands. "Nick, Allyson is pregnant for him." He grinned, then turned his head to the side. "Wait, don't tell me you knew already?"

He glanced over at someone who was walking by, then shifted his attention back to me. "Answer me. Did you know that she was pregnant?"

"Nariah...."

"Nick, you told me you'd never lie to me. Please don't be like your brother. Just tell me."

He looked down and began twisting one of his dreads.

"NICK! DID YOU KNOW THE BITCH WAS PREGNANT OR NOT?"

He pulled me by my waist, then covered my mouth with his hand.

"Chill out girl. You can't be yelling shit like that out in public. Look, I'll tell you whatever you wanna know, but this is not the place for that. You already know we can't be seen out and about like this."

"Well, where can we go? Can we go to your room? Cuz the way I'm feeling right now, it's best that I don't go back around Deron for a minute."

He stepped back from me and laughed. "How you gon' come to my room with him on the same floor? Nariah, that's not possible. We can talk about this another time."

"No one will see us Nick, so it is possible. And right now I don't care. I just need to vent."

"Aight man," he sighed. "You can't stay for longer than twenty minutes tho."

He grabbed my hand and led me back into the hotel. As we walked into the lobby, I instantly felt like there were a pair of eyes on me. I looked around, but didn't see anyone except the person at the front desk. I picked up my pace and got closer to Nick. When we made it to his room, I walked inside and sat on the edge of the bed. He closed and locked the door, then stood against the wall.

"I think we were being watched."

"What do you mean you think we were being watched? Nariah, calm down. You're not in your right state of mind. Ain't nobody was watching us except the security cameras. Now, what makes you think Allyson is pregnant?"

"I don't think it, Nick. I know it. When I got out of the shower, I went through his phone. I was lying in the bed and it kept lighting up from across the room, so I got up and got in it."

"How you get in his phone though? I know he keeps a lock on his shit."

"He does, but he unlocked it."

Nick looked at me and laughed. "How did he unlock it when he was passed out?"

"Because I... look, don't worry about that. Is Allyson pregnant or not?"

"To be real, I don't know if she's pregnant. I know that they've been in contact with each other, but I ain't heard nothing about a pregnancy. He don't really tell me shit about her."

"So you knew that they were still talking to each other, and you just didn't tell me?"

"What you mean man? That's not my place to tell you that. And at the same time, look at what we doing."

"That's not the point Nick!" I shook my head and stood up. "You tell me all the time that I deserve better, but yet you're covering for this nigga instead of letting me know that he's fucking over me!"

"Nariah, I feel you, but at the end of the day he's still my brother. I can't just throw that man in the fire like that. If I would've came at you about him and Allyson, what would you have done besides throw it in his face and start some shit? You would've confronted him about her, then what?"

"Then what? Whose side are you on???"

"It's not about sides. Some shit just don't need to be said or discussed, especially when it don't concern me."

When he said that, my eyes got big. He was acting like the shit that Deron was doing was justified. Nick stood up and walked over to me.

"You know I care about you, but I can't tell you shit that will cause you to react the way you are now without putting what we have on the line. The shit that he's doing is fucked up, but what we doing ain't right either. So you might as well just charge it to the game and let it go."

"Let it go? I'm fucking hurt! The nigga made a baby on me Nick! I can't just let it go!"I felt myself beginning to tear up again. "You know what? You're right. This was a mistake. I'm sorry for coming here. I'm just gonna g…"

Next thing you know, Nicks lips were pressed into mine. I broke the kiss and wiped my eyes.

"I can't do this Nick. I'm sorry."

"Yes you can. Don't even think about that nigga right now, bae. He fucked up cuz he don't know what he got. Let me take that pain away."

He leaned back in and kissed me, then placed his hands on my ass. My pussy was starting to get wet and I could feel his dick rising, but I was still focused on some of the things he had just said. I broke the kiss again and looked him in his eyes.

"What would you do if we ever got caught?"

"Nariah relax. Quit worrying about all of that. If it happens, we'll handle it when the time comes. But right now you ain't got nothing to worry about. Trust me."

He tilted my head to the right, then slowly ran his tongue up my neck and around my ear. I wanted to stop him, but I couldn't. My body wouldn't allow me to. I knew that what I was doing was wrong, but at the moment it felt so right. Nick had me feeling the way Deron used to make me feel… wanted.

"Lay down," he whispered in my ear.

"Why?"

"Just lay down baby. Let me take care of you."

I laid on the bed and looked up at him. This man was everything Deron used to be. He took off his clothes and licked his lips. The sight before me sent chills down my spine. His dick was hard as a rock and throbbing. He walked up to me and untied my robe, exposing my curvaceous body.

He kneeled down and lifted my legs, then placed them on his shoulder. He ran his tongue down up my entire left leg and stopped at my pussy. He looked up at me with a devilish grin.

"Try not to be too loud."

He put his dead down and began sucking on my clit.

"Mmmmmm," I moaned.

He sucked it a little harder, then began twirling his tongue all around it in a circle.

"Ahhhhh."

He licked my pussy up and down for a few seconds, then started fucking me with his tongue. Words can't describe how this man had me feeling. When I felt myself about to cum, I grabbed a handful of his dreads and began pushing his head up and down.

"MMMMMMM, NICK! I FEEL IT! I FEEL IT!"

Boom! Boom! Boom!

As soon as I was about to cum, there was a knock at the door. I pulled myself up and looked at Nick.

BOOM! BOOM! BOOM!

The knocks got louder. I jumped up off of the bed and quickly tied my robe.

"Are you expecting someone?" I asked nervously.

Nick stood up and started putting his clothed on.

"Nah, I'm not. I don't know who the fuck this could be, but I'm about to find out."

He lifted the mattress off of the bed and pulled out his gun.

"What are you doing with that?"

BOOM! BOOM! BOOM! BOOM! BOOM!

"Just get in the bathroom and lock the door. Don't come out until I tell you."

He walked up to the door and cocked his gun. "WHO IS IT?"

"Nick. It's Ariel. I need to talk to you."

I folded my arms and gave him a confused look. Ariel? What the fuck was she doing here?

TO BE CONTINUED…

CPSIA information can be obtained
at www.ICGtesting.com
Printed in the USA
LVOW10s1947190418
574122LV00013B/924/P